Restless City

Restless City

H. Lee Barnes • John H. Irsfeld
Brian Rouff • Leah Bailly
John L. Smith • Constance Ford
Vu Tran

Geoff Schumacher, Editor

CityLife Books • Las Vegas, Nevada

Cover Designer: Joslynn Anderson, member of the AIGA Las Vegas Chapter
Book Designer: Krissy Hawkins
Production Coordinator: Stacey Fott

Cataloging-in-Publication
Bailly, Leah.
  Restless city / Leah Bailly, H. Lee Barnes, Constance Ford, John Irsfeld, Brian Rouff, John L. Smith, Vu Tran ; editor, Geoff Schumacher.
  144 p. : 19 cm.
Includes author biographies.
ISBN: 1-935043-16-1 (pbk.)
ISBN: 1-935043-11-0 (ebook)
ISBN-13: 978-1-935043-16-4 (pbk.)
ISBN-13: 978-1-935043-11-9 (ebook)
  In this collaboratively written novel, each author contributes one chapter to a crime noir tale centered on Daniel Brady, a private investigator, who is investigating the death of one woman and the attempted suicide of another in Las Vegas.
1. Las Vegas (Nev.)—Fiction. 2. Mystery fiction. I. Title. II. Barnes, H. Lee. III. Ford, Constance. IV. Irsfeld, John. V. Rouff, Brian. VI. Smith, John L, VII. Tran, Vu. VII. Schumacher, Geoff, ed.
[Fic]   2009

CITYLIFE
BOOKS

An imprint of Stephens Press, LLC • P.O. Box 1600 (89125-1600)
1111 West Bonanza Road • Las Vegas, Nevada 89106
www.stephenspress.com • www.lvcitylifebooks.com
Printed in United States of America

"For a loser, Las Vegas is the meanest town on Earth."
— **Hunter S. Thompson**

CONTENTS

EDITOR'S NOTE: *Geoff Schumacher* 8

CHAPTER ONE: *H. Lee Barnes* 13

CHAPTER TWO: *John H. Irsfeld* 33

CHAPTER THREE: *Brian Rouff* 51

CHAPTER FOUR: *Leah Bailly* 67

CHAPTER FIVE: *John L. Smith* 85

CHAPTER SIX: *Constance Ford* 101

CHAPTER SEVEN: *Vu Tran* 113

AUTHOR BIOGRAPHIES: 136

Editor's Note

by

GEOFF SCHUMACHER

The organizers of the Vegas Valley Book Festival, especially Richard Hooker, got this project started. Richard and others wanted the festival to offer not only a few days of enlightening literary discussion each fall but to contribute something meaningful to the local culture. Inspired by collaborative writing projects in other cities, Las Vegas Writes was born.

I was asked to serve as the coordinator and editor of Las Vegas Writes, and with help from several local literary experts, I compiled a long list of Southern Nevada's top writers. The seven ultimately selected to participate in writing the novel, eventually titled *Restless City*, are among the best in Las Vegas. I had every confidence going in that this experiment in collaborative ficton writing would be a big success.

The process was fairly simple. Each writer was responsible for a chapter, and the chapters were written serially. So, each writer advanced the story based on what his or her predecessors had written. The only guideline I gave the writers was to maintain the general traits and history of the main characters. Beyond that, they could take the story pretty much wherever they wanted.

H. Lee Barnes went first, creating a main character, private investigator Daniel Brady, and a mystery surrounding the death of one woman and the attempted suicide of another. Through the characters and storyline of that initial chapter, Barnes clearly set the stage for *Restless City* to be a crime noir tale. The other authors followed Barnes' lead, thrusting Brady into a tangled web of intrigue that is pure Vegas.

The plot of *Restless City* is captivating enough, but what I really love are the writers' perspectives on Las Vegas, sometimes offhand comments, sometimes more elaborate commentaries.

In the first chapter, H. Lee Barnes has the private eye, Brady, ponder the Fremont Street Experience:

"The Experience looked to him like the world's largest batting cage, no view of the sky; in summer it was hot and in winter cold. He didn't even like the dancing laser light show. . . . Fremont Street was one of those changes to progress that a segment of natives to Las Vegas, Brady among them, resented."

John Irsfeld outlines a colorful legend about why Benny Binion's Horseshoe casino had some of the best Mexican food in town:

"The story was that Binion would get homesick for sure-enough good old-fashioned Tex-Mex food, *norteno* — after all, he was a Texas boy — and he'd drive to San Antonio and get him the finest Tex-Mex chef he could find, offer him a lot of money, throw him in the car, and bring him back to Las Vegas. Things would be fine for a while, the story would go, until the chef got drunk and homesick at the same time, and he would quit, tack a GTT sign on his door, and head back to San Antonio. The old man would stew about it for a while, but inevitably, back to San Antonio he'd go himself, lasso another Tex-Mex specialist, and drag him back home to Nevada."

In Brian Rouff's chapter, Brady ventures to Laughlin, where he meets with a washed-up comedian named "Germy" Boozer, who seems more interested in angering his audience than in making them laugh:

"From somewhere near the stage, a beer bottle whizzed past Boozer's head, splattering against a fake palm tree. A dumpy middle-aged couple wearing identical yellow 'Colorado River Rat' T-shirts stood up and waddled toward the door, muttering something about 'sacrilege.' A whiskey-soaked voice screamed, 'You're going to hell!' As the man behind the voice rushed the stage, two security guards wrestled him to the floor."

Leah Bailly takes Brady to the underworld of Boulder Highway, which she calls "Sketchville":

"Land of kitchenettes and weekly rentals and massage parlors with cheap boob-job quacks in the back. The sun was down completely by the time Juliet pulled up to a three-story motel, iron balcony and half-flashing sign. A heavy-gutted thug in a wife-beater and sweatpants eyed the convertible from the office doorway as they stepped out onto the street, the pavement still warm."

John L. Smith introduces some memorable new characters, including a venerable Las Vegan named Helen McGreevey:

"She was eighty, had worked at the original El Rancho Vegas for Belden Katleman in the early '50s. She broke in as an underage shill at the El Cortez when Benny Siegel took over the race wire there. At the El Rancho, she fell in love with Irish Charlie McGreevey, a skilled casino man killed by Johnny Marshall, who was of course never prosecuted for the crime. Helen was known as the first female floorman in Las Vegas. She was tougher than Tyson on cheaters and would point out card counters by ridiculing their arithmetic. 'What are you, counting with your fingers and toes?' she'd roar in her cigarette-scarred voice for everyone in the blackjack pit to hear."

Constance Ford leads Brady to the suburban mansion where the climax of this story plays out:

"A bathroom with a shiny whirlpool tub and thick towels, a room that looked like a sports bar, complete with a stripper pole and neon Budweiser signs, and beyond that, a black and red dungeon. A dungeon? He glanced in, trying to gather as many details as he could. Yes, metal restraints on the far wall, handcuffs dangling, a black padded table, a glass cabinet filled with cattails and flogs. A swing. Not exactly your ordinary Vegas mansion."

Among the seven writers, Vu Tran had the toughest task. In

taking on the final chapter, he had to make sense of everything that had transpired thus far and try to tie up as many loose ends as possible. Not surprisingly, Tran pulls it off, delivering a satisfying conclusion to this multifaceted story.

In the process, Tran creates a scene that readers won't soon forget: a poker game in which the participants — men and women, young and old — are required to play in the nude:

"Inside the windowless room, amid the sounds of Hank Williams singing 'Hey Good Lookin,' a poker game was in progress. Four young women and four older men — including the Ancient Mariner himself — were playing, and there was not a stitch of clothing in sight. The women were quite attractive, and the men were thankfully sitting down."

These are just tastes of *Restless City*, tidbits to suggest what readers can look forward to as they dive into this novel, which, amazingly, holds together quite well despite being developed by seven different writers working independently.

The Vegas Valley Book Festival, I believe, can be proud of this contribution to the local culture. I personally would like to acknowledge the following people who helped me in one way or another with this project: Richard Hooker, Georgia Neu, Suzanne Scott, Carolyn Hayes Uber, Dayvid Figler, Claudia Keelan, Shane Gammon, Andrew Kiraly, and, of course, the writers chiefly responsible for the success of this work.

Chapter One

By H. Lee Barnes

Below to the east the lights of Las Vegas stretched out to the base of Sunrise Mountain. Brady, leaning against his Ford sedan, watched Axel set the kickstand and swing his leg over the saddle. The burly biker removed his helmet and set it on the seat, then unzipped an inside vest pocket. He took a folded paper from the pocket and stared at the distant lights. Brady stepped away from the car. Only then did Axel look at him.

"Quiet out here," Brady said.

"Yeah. Time was," Axel said, "you could bring a girl out here, sit in a car and . . . Well, that's gone. No doubt they'll build some mall here. Yuppieville, that's what they've done to it."

"It was better then."

"Better 'an what? It's just Vegas. More lights now. Here, I got what you wanted. Maybe not all but . . ." Axel extended the folded paper to Brady. "Phone numbers and addresses for a few of them."

Brady slipped the paper in his shirt pocket. "How's she doing?"

Axel rubbed his jowls with his free hand. He looked behind him at the shadows of the Spring Mountain Range where a new moon hung above the ridge. "The doctor said she took five units of blood. They stitched her arms. She doesn't talk much. But at least she ain't tried nothin' stupid again."

"Well, I wish you the best."

"The best? I been prayin'. Funeral's Saturday. She'll be better after that. Least that's the hope."

"Yeah. Look, I'm still working on the money."

"Okay. It ain't so important right now. We made arrangements with the mortuary. Look, I gotta get back. Ilene's half-sister's gotta go to work. Can't leave her alone for long after what she tried." Axel faced Brady, who nodded. Then Axel pointed a finger toward the paper in Brady's pocket. "It's not about money. I mean, the money will help with the funeral. See, she loved that old woman. You make it work. Elsewise they get away with it. If I can find something else, I will."

Brady reached over and shook Axel's hand, then dropped his to his side. He felt obligated to assure Axel. "In the right hands the names will help."

Axel nodded. "Don't try my number. I'll have to call you. You know, same as before."

"Are you scared?"

"That's not somethin' I'd answer if I was."

"Right."

Brady kept his spot at the side of the road as Axel, illuminated in the headlights of an oncoming vehicle, mounted the Harley and strapped on his helmet. A pickup, its tires whistling on the pavement, sped by heading west toward Red Rock Canyon or beyond. Axel raised his hand in a salute. The pipes thundered to life and Axel swung the bike in a half circle and followed the path of the truck.

Brady turned and walked to his car. By the time he flipped on the dome light and unfolded the paper, the motorcycle was no more than a fading taillight. For him it *was* about money. Hand over the names. A payday and gone. As he read down the list of names and addresses, he recognized the first on the list, Joseph Don Walker, a thug who'd once been a union organizer, and the fourth, Andy Sachman.

Sachman he knew from the '80s before machines went electronic, before buttons and poker combinations and payout slips replaced gears and handles and images of fruit and slot trays that clattered with coin. Sachman had been a slot man, a member of a loosely linked cheating ring that took off casinos in a variety of scams ranging from setting slot jackpots to slipping coolers into blackjack games. Three in that crew had served or were still serving time. Now, cheaters were mathematicians. Card counters or computer geeks. Sachman's trade was old school, finding a machine with worn handle gears and pumping the bank dry of coins or drilling the side and setting a jackpot.

The other names were unfamiliar. Andy, he thought, most likely. He copied the names and information onto a notepad, placed that in the glove box, and stuffed the original list in his shirt pocket.

He couldn't make a connection between Walker and Sachman, except that both were slime. Still, there could be a connection. A jail cell. A dope deal. Who knows? Those types can recognize one another for what they are among a horde crowded in the stands of the Rose Bowl. Gotta be in the genes, Brady thought, some basic instinct among assholes, not unlike horses finding water in a desert. For humans like Sachman and Walker, it's the slime instinct.

He flipped off the dome light and started the engine. A sixty-seven-year-old woman, he thought, left to choke to death with a rag stuffed in her mouth. Then a granddaughter who tried suicide on pills. The random crap of the world. Well, at least now he could pass it on. It was someone else's concern. But he was cursed with curiosity, the detective's disease. He opened his cell phone, scanned the directory, and hit the call button.

"Hello, Daniel," a woman's voice said.

"Lil, I've got some more names."

"Can't help on them. I'm sitting in the 'Shoe. Come see me."

* * *

Brady parked in the lot by Fitzgerald's and walked to Fremont Street. The Experience looked to him like the world's largest batting cage, no view of the sky; in summer it was hot and in winter cold. He didn't even like the dancing laser light show. Hell, he thought as he looked up at the mesh ceiling, next they'll replace dancers and showgirls with computer images and flash them on a screen. Fremont Street was one of those changes to progress that a segment of natives to Las Vegas, Brady among them, resented. That along with the sprawl. He took small satisfaction in the fact that progress that had come so fast and so easily was backfiring on the city and things like the downtown laser show brought little tourist money.

The list Axel had given him was in his shirt pocket, but the names were circling around in his head, especially Sachman's. The old woman had been a jackpot collector for a crew. That much was certain. The names on the list may or may not be those of the ones who set up the jackpots. Brady figured she'd welched on somebody. Three-hundred-sixty thousand would be a temptation.

Brady wove his way through the crowd waiting for the laser show and stepped inside the Horseshoe. He found Lillian waiting at the bar. She lifted her glass to him as he took the seat next to her. It was obvious the drink wasn't her first of the evening. They'd met when he was a state Gaming Control Board agent working the Cooler Crew, a gang of cheaters who ran fixed decks on baccarat tables. She'd been on loan from Metro working undercover as a baccarat shill. The gang had recruited her into the scam along with the whole baccarat shift at the Dunes. Petite and pretty then. Aging now, but still sexy, he thought. He'd made a move on her when the case was over and they were celebrating at the Holy Cow. Married then, she kissed him on the cheek and told him, "Nice thought." Now, two husbands and three divorces later, she was a sergeant at the police academy and went for younger men. He didn't blame her.

"What're you drinking?"

She raised an eyebrow and grinned. "Vodka martini. I like the Tomolives."

"The what?"

"Nevermind."

The bartender laid a second martini in front of her and reached for the first.

"Leave it, Tommy," she said. "I eat the Tomolives."

Brady looked at the pearl-shaped vegetable in the glass and understood.

"Tommy, this is Daniel. He probably wants a Coke."

Tommy wiped his hand on a towel and shook Brady's hand. "Pleased. So, a Coke?"

"Diet. With a lemon squeeze."

"Diet with lemon." The bartender gave Lillian a sly grin and turned away. Lillian used a toothpick to spear the Tomolive from the glass. She let it rest in her teeth for an instant, then chewed and swallowed it. "Love 'em. So, Dan, how are you?"

"All and all, okay. Still got that gorgeous red hair."

"'Cept now I have to use dye to cover the gray. Happens."

Tommy set the Coke down before Brady. "Enjoy," he said and grinned. "If you need a cab later, let me know."

Lillian chuckled and raised her martini. "To the old days."

"To them. So, what did you dig up?"

"Are you going to tell me what this is about?"

"I can't yet. It's . . . I have to keep this confidential."

"Sure, confidential. Does my department have a case going on this?"

"I can't say."

"I'll assume it does."

She leaned close to him. "You know I could be brought up on charges for doing this?"

"Old friends having a drink?"

"You don't drink."

"Right. No one'll charge you for what's not mentioned."

Lillian smirked. "It's not like the old days. When I joined, there were guys left over from the Intelligence Task Force who'd beat the crap out of pimps and pushers and run them out of town. Remember them?"

"Yeah. Maybe it's better now."

"Money's better. Anyhow, your James Allen Axelrod has two convictions. Possession of a controlled substance with intent to distribute and another for battery with a deadly weapon. My man in Intelligence tells me he left the outlaw life, had his tattoos cut off, and joined a Christian motorcycle club. Lives in Blue Diamond."

"That fits. His girlfriend?"

"The woman who tried suicide?"

"Yeah, I guess I left that girlfriend part out."

"I'm guessing you left a lot out. I'm guessing you don't want the cops involved."

"Like you said, you're guessing."

"Don't let this backfire in my face, Dan."

"It won't."

"Ilene Georgia Davies, nothing but work applications. She's currently a dealer at Red Rock Station. Lives in the southwest off Russell Road, one of those half-sold developments." Lillian took a sip from her drink and winked at Brady. "Daniel Brady. And why couldn't you be fifteen years younger?"

"Age keeps me outta trouble."

"No going back, is there? Well, as for your other name, Quinton Lee Samuels. He's got no record here. Only three traffic citations in Orange County. What I did find out is he's a high-roller, something I imagine you already knew. Is he your payday?"

Brady smiled and downed half his Coke. He pulled a hundred out and placed it atop the bar.

"What's that?" Lillian asked.

"Two more drinks and cab fare home."

"Well, it's nice to know you care."

"Thanks. I gotta go."

"Brady?"

"Yes."

"Kiss me before you go." She presented him her cheek.

He kissed her and squeezed her shoulder.

"This was for old times," she said. "We put that whole gang away, didn't we?"

"Every asshole and the dealers and bosses. Best attorneys in town didn't crack you on the stand."

"Hell, two of them tried to date me afterward. But I was married."

"I remember. Take it easy and have Tommy call you a cab."

* * *

Brady pressed the button to the penthouse suites. He wondered what a penthouse suite ran a night. It wasn't likely that

Samuels got a bill for it. Lillian said he was a high-roller, but to be entitled to a suite like this he had to be a whale. When the doors opened, he looked up at the camera. Everywhere, he thought, electronic eyes. That's what the casinos depended on these days. Gone, the reformed cross-roaders who once manned the eyes in the sky and the spotters who patrolled the slot aisles. He remembered when the casinos wouldn't use computers. Now they track play with them, and of course, cameras.

At the top floor, he knocked on the third door on the left. The door cracked open and a young man exposing half his face gazed out. He nodded and opened the door. Tall, dark haired, neatly dressed in a gray three-button suit and clean shaven, he had the look of a college athlete. Not a football player, more the lacrosse type, Brady thought.

"Mr. Samuels is out on the deck." He pointed to the sliding glass doors. "Would you like a drink of some kind?"

"Water will do. Tap's fine with me. No ice."

Samuels looked over his shoulder as Brady slid the door open. "I like promptness, Mr. Brady."

"Yes, sir. I had to meet someone to get information."

"Well, we meet face to face at last." Samuels stood and offered his hand. He was at least two inches taller than Brady, six-foot-four, perhaps six-five, and slender. His hair was silver gray and wavy. He wore a red Fila tennis shirt, white shorts, and sandals. "Have a seat, Mr. Brady. Did Kevin offer you a drink?"

"Yes, sir."

Samuels held up a half-full wine glass. "Malbec, from Mendoza Valley. You should try it."

"Thank you, sir. I don't drink."

"Was it John Wayne who said he didn't trust a man who didn't drink or a woman who did?"

"I don't know."

"I guess we'll get to business. You seem that type, Mr. Brady. What do you have for me?"

"Names. A few addresses." Brady took the list from his pocket and handed it over.

Samuels looked over the list, nodded, and turned back to Brady. "Would you say he's a reliable source?"

"I have no reason to doubt him."

"Did you copy these down somewhere?"

"Sir?"

"The names, did you copy them?"

"No."

"I paid you for names. That was our arrangement. You were to get names, nothing more. Unless I decided. And you're to forget this came to my possession."

"Yes, sir. Something else. The granddaughter, Ilene, the one who tried suicide?"

"I know who she is. Yes, what about her?"

"She doesn't have enough money for the funeral. Her boyfriend wanted to know if . . ."

"Assure them I'll take care of any funeral expenses, anonymously, of course. I don't feel comfortable giving money to . . . You said he was an outlaw biker, right?"

"He was an outlaw. Apparently he's a born again, belongs to one of those Christian biker clubs now."

"Christian bikers? Makes one wonder."

Kevin stepped out on the balcony. He handed Brady the glass of water and turned to Samuels. "Do you need anything else, sir?"

"Yes, I want you to search Mr. Brady here. Mr. Brady, if you would stand."

"What am I looking for?" Kevin asked.

"A piece of paper with some names on it. A list."

Brady stood as asked while Kevin reached in his pockets and emptied the contents of each on the table. When Kevin was finished, a wallet, car keys, two pens, a money clip with four $100 bills and some loose change lay atop the table. Kevin thumbed through the address book and handed it to his boss.

"Kevin," Samuels said as he looked through the address book, "has an MBA from Stanford. Entry-level jobs are few these days. He auditioned for 'The Apprentice,' but Trump didn't find him suitable. Sad state of affairs." He laid the address book back on the table. "You can go, Kevin. Have a seat, Mr. Brady."

Brady settled into the chair. Below to the east the Strip was teaming with traffic, cars backed up from Tropicana Avenue to Desert Inn Road. The restless city, Brady thought. People chasing dreams in slow motion. He drank from the glass and held it between his hands. Finish the glass, get your money, and excuse yourself, Brady thought. He drank the remaining water and stood.

"Well, I guess that's it then?" he said.

"Relax. Stay and enjoy the view. Isn't it odd how quiet it is up here? All those cars, but silence here."

Brady wasn't into chitchat. He wanted his pay and to take his leave. "Quiet. Really, I should be going."

"Kevin has an envelope waiting. Bonus money in it as well. Now, I'm paying you very well, Mr. Brady. Please indulge me."

They sat silently the better part of five minutes, Samuels sipping occasionally from his wine glass, Brady staring off, uncomfortable, anxious to leave. Then Samuels downed the last of the wine, walked to the balustrade, and shattered the glass. It splintered into shards, most of which flew over the face of the hotel. He smiled at Brady and went to the sliding door.

"Kevin, I'll be needing another glass," he said and closed the doors.

When Kevin came, he brought a wine glass, broom, and a broom pan as if this were a common occurrence. He swept up the broken glass and left. Samuels sat and poured himself a fresh glass from the bottle.

"An old man can't punch walls," he said.

"Probably not," Brady said.

"The dead woman," Samuels said and went silent.

Brady waited a minute before saying her name. "Colleen Winters."

"Winters, Moore, Harrison," Samuels said. "She married three times. Her maiden name was Colleen Depeau. Cajun. When I met her, she was twenty-seven, divorced, and had a daughter nine. The girl's name was Lenore. She died four years ago from cancer.

"As I said — no, I guess I didn't yet — Colleen was beautiful. She was a baccarat shill at the Sands. In some casinos back then it was the same as being a house girl for high-rollers. I had made a lot of money as real estate boomed in Los Angeles. I saw the future, you might say. At thirty I was a multimillionaire. I'm not saying this to brag. I took a chance and came up lucky. So I met Colleen.

"I loved her. She, I like to believe, loved me. But I was married, two children, two boys. Too much was at stake for me to leave my family. The divorce might have cost twenty million. So it was weekends in Las Vegas. What do you know about 1969, Mr. Brady?"

"Not much. I was ten. Woodstock, I guess."

"Yes, Woodstock. Young people trapped in filth on a farm. No toilets."

"Really?"

"You see, history is a matter not just of experience but who interprets it. The press has turned the era into a dreamland of love among flower children. I lost a younger sister, one of the flower children, to hepatitis. A dirty needle, bad water, some other contact with the disease. She, like myself, came from money. She rejected it.

"By 1969, I was earning millions, with more to come. Along the way, I'd married a woman I didn't love and had two sons."

Brady's cell phone vibrated. He looked at the display.

"Am I boring you, Mr. Brady?"

Brady returned the phone to its holster. "No, sir. Sorry."

"The flower children disappeared, replaced now as we see by cell-phone children. Quite a shift in two generations. Maybe I'm just old. I'm seventy-two now. But to Colleen. I spent lavishly on her. It wasn't what she wanted. She wanted a family. I wanted her to myself when I wanted her. You see, I couldn't divorce. I loved my sons and truth is, I valued money too much to give it to . . . I stayed with my wife. Four years, Colleen and I kept our affair going. I knew my wife suspected, but figured it meant nothing. She, ah, had long seemed indifferent to whatever I did."

Samuels poured a fresh glass of wine and leaned back. Brady listened, but he was impatient to leave. He'd heard enough to fill in the blanks. It was a common story. He played it through in his mind to the inevitable end. Loss years before. Regrets now.

Some way to make amends. Samuels held the glass to his nose and inhaled, took a drink. He looked. His mouth went slack as he disappeared into thought.

"So, why did it end five years later?"

"Why? Money. Plain and simple. Yes." Samuels took a sip and set the glass aside. "My wife hired one of your kind. My activity in Vegas wasn't hard to track. I was open about us, took her to dinner at the Bacchanal Room, the Dome of the Sea. I even took her gambling. They got photos of us. None in the casinos, of course, because . . . you know why. Anyhow, my wife threatened me with divorce. She wanted the boys, all of the property, most of the money, half the business. It was early 1974 then, a rough year. My sister died that year, the hepatitis, so did our mother, a stroke. The year was my Watergate, sort of. Caught cold, no chance of covering it up.

"Guilt is a powerful force in our lives. For the moral man, anyhow. I never divorced. I agreed to cease all contact with Colleen. I did, however, hire an attorney who for a time kept watch for me. I funneled money to her through him until he died.

"Age, Mr. Brady. She became a grandmother and gambler. Got into debt. I wasn't there to help. As I said, guilt is a powerful force. When word came how she died, I flew up. The attorney I hired recommended you to make the inquiries. Said you were discreet. Are you, Mr. Brady?"

"Yes."

"Is it true she was collecting illegal jackpots for a gang, as the police report claims?"

"Yes. She was what we call a claimer. Another agency, one that tracks this type of activity for the casinos, had her in photos, claiming over fifteen jackpots. Money ranged from eighteen thousand to just under seventy thousand over two years. Total figure nearly a quarter million. Then a big one, three hundred sixty big."

"How long ago was that?"

"Two months before her . . ."

"These names, do you know any?"

"Two."

"Are they cheats?"

"Cheaters? One yes. Sachman."

Samuels took a drink of wine, set the glass aside, and spread open the list. He turned so the paper caught light through the sliding glass door. "Andrew Sachman. How old is he?"

"Mid-fifties."

"Would he kill someone if he suspected she would put him in prison?"

"You're not telling me something?" Brady's other contacts at Metro had mentioned nothing about her being a potential witness.

"You used to be a cop, you can figure it out."

Brady nodded. "Gaming Control agent, actually. I don't know

if he would. Did you hire someone else as well?"

"I employed an attorney. What he discovered is another matter. If I pay you, can you find out about Sachman? Or if not him, who?"

"Find out." Brady looked at the Strip, still jammed with cars. He sighed. "You should let the police handle it."

"Yes, I should. Answer my question, can you?"

"Honestly, I don't know." Brady's cell phone vibrated again. He looked at the incoming number, the same as the last call. "Excuse me. I should take this."

"Go ahead."

Brady went to the balustrade. His back to Samuels, he pressed the talk button. "Hello, Brady here."

"Yes. You don't know me. I'm Ilene's sister. I was told to call this number if anything happened."

Brady cupped the phone and said, "Is Ilene okay?"

"Yes. Well, sort of. I haven't told her yet."

"Told her what?"

"Her boyfriend called me and said he was coming but had to stop somewhere for a few minutes. He knew I had to go to work. It's not like Axel to hang me up. It was two hours ago, and he won't answer his phone. I've tried and tried. He gave me this number, said to call you if something. . . . Do you know where he is?"

Brady's mouth went dry. He licked his lips. "No. You should

call the police."

"He said I shouldn't unless Ilene . . . I guess I should."

"Hold on." Brady placed the phone on mute and turned to Samuels. "Mr. Samuels, the boyfriend, Axelrod, he's disappeared."

Just then the sliding glass door slid open and Kevin poked his head out. "Sir, some detectives from Metro are here. They want to talk with you."

Chapter Two

BY JOHN H. IRSFELD

Samuels looked at Brady as if it were Brady's fault that a pair of detectives was interrupting their conversation, as if the murder of an old girlfriend was nobody's business but theirs, and certainly not the cops'.

For unknown reasons, Brady felt a tinge of guilt, as if he had indeed called the cops and told them that Samuels was in town and had a connection with the front page — but below the fold — story of a brutal murder. As if there were any other kind.

Almost against his will, Brady shrugged. Then he and Samuels both stood.

"Bring them out here, won't you, Kevin? Don't bring any extra chairs. They won't be long."

"Yes, sir," Kevin said, no emotion reflected either in his voice or on his face.

A moment later, Kevin ushered two young men, or so they seemed to Brady, out the sliding door to the deck.

"Thank you, Kevin," Samuels said. "That will be all. I'll call you if I need you."

Brady wondered. Why would a Stanford MBA take such a job? If he was a Stanford MBA. Well, money talks. It spoke to Brady.

"Mr. Samuels?" one of the young detectives said. "I know it ain't you," he said then to Brady. Brady smiled slightly.

"Yes?" Mr. Samuels said, apparently no longer perturbed by the interruption. Well, thought Brady, you don't get to be a whale by spouting off when the whalers come around.

"I'm Detective Brittain," said the young man. "Two t's. This is my partner, Detective McCullough." He extended his hand, which Mr. Samuels ignored. In a moment Brittain's hand fluttered down to his side. As for McCullough, he only nodded, as if he'd seen this movie before and didn't want to sit through it again.

"Please, have a seat," Brittain said.

"Will this take that long?" Samuels asked.

"That's pretty much up to you, Mr. Samuels," Brittain said. "And your buddy Brady here."

Brady half smiled again. He knew he should have taken the

money and run when he had the chance. If he had had the chance. He decided to sit. This could take as long as the two young cops wanted it to take and it could be as uncomfortable as they wanted it to be. Samuels hadn't exactly started the meeting off the way Brady would have advised, but rich people, they really are different from you and me, and it ain't just because they've got more money, either. They know God has touched them and made them one of His own — He loves them best, or they wouldn't be rich.

So, although Brady sat, Samuels did not. Even in his Fila tennis outfit and sandals, he was an imposing figure, taller by half a foot than either of Metro's finest, and enhanced, as some lucky men are, by the silver of his age.

"We wanted to ask you a few questions about Colleen Winters," Detective Brittain said.

"And why would you think I know anything about this Colleen Winters?"

"Look. We can make this easy or we can make this hard. That's your call." It wasn't a question. "Colleen Winters, nee Colleen Depeau, an old girlfriend of yours from some forty years ago, found dead in her house here in Metroland several days ago, done in with a rag shoved halfway down her throat and a few little marks on her body inflicted by someone who apparently wanted to make an impression on her. Like maybe they wanted to know something she wouldn't tell them."

Detective McCullough laughed. "And we know," McCullough said, "that very soon after she died, you left your home over in paradise and came back here to your old playground."

"Coincidence?" said Detective Brittain. "Down at Metro, we concluded that the answer to that was 'No.' We concluded that while it is true that blood is thicker than water, semen is thicker than blood. We concluded that you either knew something about this sad matter, or planned to know something about it, one."

Detective McCullough backed to the sliding glass door leading inside and leaned against the wall next to it. Like Brittain, he was wearing khaki pants, a dark polo shirt, untucked and cut fuller on the right side than the left, and well-used running shoes. Both men had plastic-encased I.D.s around their necks on dogtag chains. Both were as clean-shaven as Kevin himself, and both had short hair. Textbook stuff. Brady could see the ill-concealed lumps where their holstered pistols rode. Probably Glocks. Trendy as a Starbucks.

Brady didn't recognize either of the men, but he recognized the type. He was pretty sure he had not run across either of them since he'd taken up private work. He was also pretty sure they knew who he was, because before they had left their office someone had told them he would be there on the deck or in the TV room or somewhere in the whale's part of the ocean visiting with Samuels. The men reminded him of new guys to the team, guys who hadn't yet gotten the "quiet" part of "the quiet professionals." The name itself made Brady cringe, but he had to admit there was a part of him that was proud he had been among their number. And these two had no doubt been told the story of how Brady had lost his job at Gaming Control. Unsound practices, they had said, and although it was Brady's partner who had indulged in such practices, they both had paid the price. Sometimes "quiet" meant "silence."

He felt his phone vibrate again, but even though he was curious — Ilene's sister with information about Axel? Lil sending him a tardy heads-up? Gaming Control with an offer to return to the fold, no hard feelings? — he thought it prudent to leave it in his pocket where he'd slipped it after the earlier call.

The glass door slid open and Kevin stepped out. He was carrying a cell phone that he handed to Samuels. "It's for you, sir," he said. "Mr. Creamer."

"Please excuse me a moment, won't you?" said Samuels to the detectives. He was past showing anything now — he was the poker-playing real estate tycoon, getting ready to do whatever it was he was getting ready to do but not tipping his hand except to say, unnecessarily, "Mr. Creamer is my lawyer."

Well, thought Brady, what's the point of being really rich if you didn't have your own snitches? And anyway, what had Samuels done to anyone, except what all sociopaths do: rip them off, fuck them dry, and then kick them to the curb. I mean, he wasn't as guilty as some. Probably. Maybe.

Samuels followed Kevin off the deck and into the tastefully opulent suite. He really must lose a lot of money in this joint, Brady thought.

"So," McCullough said from his perch by the door. "How did you and Samuels get together, Brady?"

"He's an old college friend," Brady said.

"He's got twenty years on you," Brittain said.

"I said 'old,' " Brady said. "Same school, different classes."

"Very funny," McCullough said, pushing himself back from the wall and crossing to the balustrade to look out over the city. "There's two million stories in this city. And one or two of them is right here in this penthouse."

"Look," Brady said. "I did some investigating for Samuels. I reported to him the results of my investigation. We were visiting with each other. Small talk. We had just reached the part where I got paid when you two showed up. Anything beyond that, I think you ought to get from Mr. Samuels."

"You know it doesn't have to happen like this, Brady," McCullough said.

"We can take you with us when we leave, even if we can't take him," said Brittain. "Like we said, hard or easy, easy or hard. Danny."

"Let's start with Mr. Samuels, can we do that?" Brady said. "And if that doesn't get us anyplace, then we can figure out where to go after that."

Samuels returned to the deck just then. He handed the cell phone to Detective Brittain.

"Yeah," Brittain said into the phone. "Un huh. I know. Whatever you say, Mr. Creamer. Absolutely. But you know, it doesn't end here."

He nodded as he spoke, affirming or negating, it was hard to tell, but after a few moments he handed the phone back to Samuels.

"Yes?" Samuels said. "Yes, I think they are just leaving." He gently closed the clam shell. He had a contented look on his face.

"We are," said Brittain. "But we may be back. If not us, somebody. Because this conversation isn't over."

"Unfortunately for you," said Samuels, "I think it is."

Kevin appeared just then, as if he'd gotten buzzed telepathically.

"Would you show these gentlemen to the door?" Samuels said politely.

"This way, gentlemen," Kevin said, just as politely.

At the sliding door, McCullough stutter-stepped, turned back, and said to Brady, "It's guaranteed we'll see you later, though, buddy. Sure enough."

As soon as they were gone, Brady took his own cell phone out, opened it, and checked the number from the vibrating call he had not answered when the detectives were present. It was Lillian.

Brady pressed the dial key to call her back. In a moment, a man answered the phone. "Yeah?" he said.

"Lil?" said Brady foolishly.

"Who is this?" said the man at the other end of the invisible line.

"Who is *this*?" Brady said.

Whoever it was — maybe Tommy, Brady couldn't tell, maybe not — hit the end button, and that was that.

"The sister?" said Samuels.

"No," said Brady. "Not the sister. Nothing." He paused a minute and then he said, "I need to go, Mr. Samuels."

"And you would like your money," Samuels added.

Brady nodded. He couldn't check out of this joint too soon.

Again, Kevin appeared at the door.

"Please give Mr. Brady his envelope, will you, Kevin?" Samuels said.

"Yes, sir," said Kevin, again opening the door wide enough for Brady to pass by him into the suite.

* * *

On the way down, Brady examined the elevator. He would wait until he was in the Ford before he took a look at what was inside the envelope. He might even wait until he got home. He certainly didn't need to have it on the hotel tape. Right now, he could tell he was getting a headache. Two Diet Cokes was two too many late in the day. Caffeine intolerance. Goes with age. But as for going home, maybe there were better places to go right then. Still, home was the where the heart was, wasn't it? Isn't it?

He stopped the elevator at the mezzanine and took the stairs down the rest of the way. Some hotels were engineered to keep such a subterfuge from happening. Someone might have dropped the ball on this one.

He could see neither Brittain nor McCullough, but Brady knew that didn't mean they couldn't see him.

In short order, even given the insanely dense and frenetic traffic, Brady was back at the Horseshoe. Wherever Lil was, it wasn't like her not to answer her cell, especially if she could see it was Brady calling. Something was seriously off here.

He went straight to the bar — shaped like a horseshoe, of course — scanning it as he approached. No sign of Lil. No sign of Tommy. It was busier now than before, and it took him longer than he wished before the bartender slapped a napkin down in front of him, smiled and said, "And what will it be for you, buddy?"

"I'm looking for a friend," Brady said, ignoring the "buddy."

"Ain't we all," said the bartender, "ain't we all?" Men seated on both sides of Brady chuckled appreciatively. Everybody loves a comedian.

"Where's Tommy?" Brady asked.

"Who?" said the bartender.

"The guy who was on the shift before you. The bartender. Tommy."

"There ain't nobody works here named Tommy," the bartender said.

"Yes," said Brady. Well, he thought, this was beginning to look like it would get worse before it got better.

"You want something to drink or what?" the bartender said.

Brady waved him off.

As he half backed away from the bar, he saw the bartender say something to the two guys who had laughed at his earlier joke, but this time Brady couldn't hear what it was. The two guys laughed again, this time a little harder.

Brady decided to wait it out a little, see what he could come up with. Sometimes the best thing to do was nothing. Sometimes things just happened. He had not opened the envelope on the ride over, but he liked the feel of it — fat. He decided to head downstairs to the coffee shop and get something to eat. Maybe it wasn't too late to stifle the headache he could feel still building, as if it was going to go serious on him.

The gal at the hostess stand met him with a broad, bright smile and a handful of giant glossy menus. "Are you alone, sir?" she asked.

Alone, he thought. Yeah, pretty much. "Yes," he said. "Just one."

She led him to one of the few open tables. He pointed to a booth. "How about over there?" he said.

"But . . ."

"It's okay," Brady said. "I'll make up for it."

"Well . . ." she said.

But by then he was already sliding into the seat on the side facing the stairs down from the casino and the elevator up to the garage. His car was parked there, level four. Pretty good place for such a night, but then the Fremont Street Experience had its own parking garage. That whole thing, the Fremont Street Experience. What about back in the day, when they all made the loop, a weekend tribal ritual, dying even then, Charleston to Fifth, or farther, to Fremont to Main to Charleston, or maybe the other way, around and around, looking for one another and who knew what might transpire. In those days, it really was an experience. Hot nights, windows down, cars full, waving, shouting, smiling, emerging, entering, going off into the night. Now it wasn't an experience, it was just a show. They weren't the same thing.

Yet there was still Binion's, even if the old man was gone, Ted too, the daughter and her husband out of the business, and Jack back on the Mississippi River someplace. It had been something. Binion's had the Mexican food. The Four Queens had one of the best steak joints in town, downstairs in a bunker, the best newsstand in town right behind it, across from the . . . . What was the name of the theater where Brady had seen *The Last Picture Show* when it first came to town when he was a kid? *The Last Picture Show*! He hadn't really understood the movie, probably the last one he saw in a theater in black and white, but he liked it because it was kids like himself who played the big parts in it. Movies. When had he seen one last? Some things were passing him by.

Even though there were a lot of Mexican restaurants in Las Vegas now, Binion's had some of the best Mexican food Brady knew of. The story was that Binion would get homesick for sure-enough good old-fashioned Tex-Mex food, *norteno* — after all, he was a Texas boy — and he'd drive to San Antonio and get him the finest Tex-Mex chef he could find, offer him a lot of money, throw him in the car, and bring him back to Las Vegas. Things would be fine for a while, the story would go, until the chef got drunk and homesick at the same time, and he would quit, tack a GTT sign on his door, and head back to San Antonio. The old man would stew about it for a while, but inevitably, back to San Antonio he'd go himself, lasso another Tex-Mex specialist, and drag him back home to Nevada. Brady didn't know if it was true — half the stories you heard about Benny Binion he figured weren't true — but it was hard to tell which ones were and which ones weren't. It didn't matter. Maybe the cook they had now was cut out of that old Benny Binion cloth. Maybe he was even from San Antonio.

His waitress brought the food. It was okay, but it wasn't as good as it was the last time Brady had eaten there. Maybe that cook had gone to Texas and Brady was eating frozen. What did he know? He wasn't a foodie, after all. He ate only because he had to. Whatever this was, it filled the hole.

So who had answered Lil's phone? Where was Tommy? *Who* was Tommy? Was he a cop, too, who worked with Lillian and was just playing the part of bartender while they were doing whatever they were doing? Probably not. Lil was already too drunk to be on duty and, anyway, she worked exclusively at the academy these days. She wasn't ever on the street like in the old days, loaned out in the great fight against crime. Tommy was young enough, however; maybe he was Lil's date for the evening. Ah, these kids.

Just then Brady's mobile began vibrating again. He slid it out, flipped it open, and looked at the tiny screen. Not Lil and, the best he could remember, not Ilene's sister, either. Not Samuels. Who then? He pressed the talk button.

"Yes," he said.

"If you want to see anybody alive again, you'd better take your ill-gotten gains, go upstairs to that old piece of shit Ford of yours, and head down to Laughlin. Otherwise, you're out of luck, buddy." No click, just the whirr of the ether or whatever it was that carried the words through the air, and then what passed for silence on cell phones.

"Buddy?" Brady said. Or maybe he had said Brady, he wasn't sure. Well, this was a new wrinkle. So much for going home.

From his jacket, he pulled the plump envelope that Kevin had given him in Samuels' place, held it under the edge of the tabletop, ran his finger under the flap and opened it — gave himself a little paper cut doing it — and peeked inside. Not bad. Even if they were all one-dollar bills, not bad. They weren't. He inched one of the hundreds out of the envelope and put it on the table in front of him. "God damn," he said barely aloud. "Nice payday. Too bad it ain't over yet."

* * *

He hadn't been to Laughlin in a long time; not long enough, though, really — Laughlin is not the center of the universe. Didn't used to be, anyway. But off he went out on U.S. 93/95 toward Arizona, the real West. Henderson would have been a blur of salmon-tiled rooftops had it been daylight to see, not the smoky industrial trap it used to be in the days of his youth. As it was, lights, lights, and more lights. The joke used to be that at Christmas, all the locals in the valley turned off all the lights except the red and green ones. Not anymore — strip mall signs, and stoplights, and window lights burning for the return of the person who had turned them on in the first place when they'd left. Brady didn't leave the lights on when he left his place. Sometimes he didn't turn them on when he was there. It was always dark when he came back, too.

Was it Axel? Back in his old life — if it was his old life, before he was born again — Axel no doubt had made the Laughlin River Run on his Harley, back before the laser had done damage to his tattoos just as the Bible had to his sinning ways. Back before the rumble there a couple of years ago diminished the bike traffic somewhat. Axel was still rough cut, and he hadn't traded his Harley away, either. Generally, once a man had a Harley he pretty much did his best to keep it, unless a woman intervened. Brady didn't know much about Ilene except that she had both cut herself and swallowed a handful of bad pills and still had managed to live through it. Apparently she loved her Grandmother Colleen a lot — maybe even more than she loved Axel. Or maybe love didn't have anything to do with it. Maybe Ilene had something else on her mind besides grief over the loss of old granny. It sucks to be cynical, but it's safe.

Or was it Lillian, confused maybe, by love or sex, into compromising something more than her body? It couldn't be Samuels. He was safe in his aerie with Kevin. MBA, my ass, Brady thought. It couldn't be Ilene, of course. She was already in trouble enough of her own making. And as for old Colleen, she had already been done in. So who?

And why was he making this trip anyway? He had taken a

job, done the job, gotten paid for the job, eaten a passably good Mexican meal, paid for it with cash, and then tipped well, and should already be at home either in bed or poking around in his medicine cabinet looking for a Motrin or Excedrin or his house gun or something to stop the niggling, nagging, painful beat of the persistent ache behind his eyes.

Brady slowed down at the Railroad Pass casino to make sure no unhappy loser decided just then to pull into oncoming traffic so he wouldn't have to go home and try to explain to a significant other where all the money had gone. Brady was safe — his way was clear. Not much farther on, he pulled off 93/95 on to plain old 95, Veterans Memorial Highway, on his way south toward the cutoff to 163 east that took any curious soul into Laughlin, then on to Bullhead City, Arizona, too, if he wanted to go there — if that curious soul turned out to be as bull-headed as maybe Brady was starting to seem even to himself.

Veterans Memorial Highway. Brady guessed they couldn't have found a lonelier, more godforsaken highway in Nevada to dedicate to veterans. Maybe they were thinking of guys like Brady when they chose this stretch of 95 to dedicate.

On impulse, Brady reached across to the glove box of the Ford and popped it open. There was his Browning, safe as a baby in its bed, sitting atop his insurance and registration papers. But where was the list with all the names on it that Axel had given him only hours before?

Brady pulled off on to the narrow emergency lane, felt the jolt of rumble strips all the way up his spine and into his aching head. He slipped the car into park, unbuckled his seat belt so he could get a closer look at the glove box, took out the Browning and the car papers, and found himself looking into a bare, poorly lit, absolutely empty cavity. No list. His head was pounding now.

"If I was ten years younger," Brady said, "I'd start to be getting pissed off just about now. And if I was ten years older, I'd be at home in bed."

Chapter Three

"Oh, this is sure stirring up some ghosts for me."
— **Robbie Robertson**

By Brian Rouff

Fourteen thousand dollars. *Waaay* too much money for a job like this. Or what the job was supposed to be when Brady signed on.

How did Samuels decide on that particular figure anyway? Didn't he believe in rounding to the next highest number? Maybe he found the dough lodged between the cushions of his Italian leather sofa.

Nah, a guy like Samuels was careful, everything planned to the nth degree. He knew exactly what he was paying for, what it was worth to him. The money was for product already received. But more importantly, for product expected. What that might be, Brady could only guess. At the moment, all he knew was that Samuels possessed the list and he didn't. His personal ace in the hole, gone missing in less than an hour. Impressive, even by Brady's standards.

One thing for sure: The money came with strings attached. Samuels would want to make damn certain he got a good return on his investment. Bigwigs like Samuels and his MBA lapdog, Kevin, didn't believe in loss leaders. Like the corporate philosophy that had sucked the life out of the casino business, every department had to show a profit. The way things stacked up, Brady knew the fourteen grand wouldn't be nearly enough. That's what happens when you get into bed with a Samuels. Who was it that said, "You lie down with dogs, you get up with fleas?" Unconsciously, Brady scratched his forehead.

A smart man would have taken the money, holed up in a four-star hotel on a tropical beach, rented a girlfriend for the week. A smart man would have options. Brady just continued to push the car south toward Laughlin. Outside, the scenery rushed past in a mind-numbing blur of desert sameness. Shrub, rock, hill. Shrub, rock, hill. Bad animation come to life.

These thoughts and a hundred others pinballed around Brady's brain, occasionally lighting up a random synapse but more often dropping into a black hole. Samuels might be the least of his worries, at that. Gravel Voice on the other end of the phone said something about not seeing anyone alive again. Pretty open-ended, that kind of threat. Who, exactly? Axel? No sweat off

Brady's balls. The biker knew what he was getting into. Tommy? Wouldn't recognize the man if he was sitting next to him in the passenger's seat. Lil? Okay, that might be a problem.

Too many loose ends. Brady hated them. His life might be in the crapper but at least it was a tidy crapper. Brady remembered a sign hanging in his old Valley High School wood shop: "When in doubt, follow directions." He didn't understand it then; he understood it now. He could do that for a while. Until something better came along.

Orange construction barrels narrowed the blacktop to one lane. Brady came up on a big fifth-wheel doing forty-five, forcing him to make a quick decision: slow down or pass. Inching into the oncoming lane, he stomped on the pedal. Instead of the burst of speed he needed, the engine serenaded him with a metallic *ping, ping, ping*, a symphony of cheap gas and neglect. Brady backed off the pedal, resolved to bide his time behind the rig, hoping it eventually would pull off to the side. A metaphor for his life, ceding control to others.

The Ford had been a lemon from the moment he drove it off the lot on East Sahara. Nine years ago, back when it was still important to buy American. A block away from the dealership, he hit a pothole and the glove box flew open. He should have flipped a U-ey and returned the piece of shit then and there. He should have done a lot of things.

Brady had never been a patient man, but he was learning.

He knew that in front of the RV was another, longer RV. And another. And another. A caravan of old-timers drawn to Laughlin's $39-per-night package deals like lemmings to a cliff. He took a deep breath and settled back into his seat. It was going to be a long ninety miles; a long time to be inside his own head.

Christ, his head pounded worse than ever, the throbbing eye pain migrating to his temples and down his jaw. Some sort of warning sign, he remembered reading long ago. Heart attack? Stroke? Brady hadn't been to a doctor in two decades, the last visit for a flu shot. It was the only time he ever got sick. He reached up and massaged his jaw. He'd have to stop in Searchlight to take a leak and pick up some aspirin and gum. That's about all that town was good for.

Brady switched on the radio, recognized Sammy Hagar in mid-yelp. "I Can't Drive 55." Appropriate. Sometimes, he felt as if the radio spoke directly to him. The thoughts of a madman, to be sure. He kept it to himself. Brady shook his head as if to clear away the notion. He and Hagar were both too old for this shit. Time for a follow-up: "I Can't *Be* 55."

Searchlight was known for two things: It was the birthplace of Nevada's senior U.S. senator, Harry Reid, and it featured quite possibly the worst speed trap in the state. Speed limits dropped precipitously from 65 to 45 to 35 to 25 in less than a quarter-mile. A flashing sign warned, "Speed Limit Strictly Enforced." No kidding. Brady figured most of the city's revenue came directly from speeders whose reflexes didn't kick in fast enough. Nevada Highway Patrol cruisers, like big, blue cheetahs, lay in wait to cut the next victim from the traffic herd.

NHP officers were the second-class citizens of Nevada law enforcement and they knew it. On average, they made about twenty thousand a year less than their Las Vegas Metropolitan Police Department counterparts. All of them gave you attitude, swaggering around and patting their gun butts while calling you "Sir" with mocking politeness.

Back when Brady came *this close* to becoming a cop himself, back when he was young and idealistic and thought he could make a difference, the joke was, "What do NHP and Metro officers have in common? They both applied for Metro."

A week away from graduation, a pit stop at the old Silver Saddle Saloon on East Charleston ended that idea forever, a couple of good old boys taking exception to Brady's tan training uniform.

"What are you supposed to be, some kind of Eagle Scout?" the bigger one asked, so far up in Brady's grill he could smell the decayed teeth and dollar beer. "Where's your merit badge, sonny?"

The smaller one chimed in, "Looks more like a Brownie, don't he, Lou?"

Brady's instincts were good back then, sharp. He knew, *knew*, that the only way out of that bar was through these morons.

When he wrapped his pool cue across the big guy's mouth, blood gushed like water from a New Orleans levee. Before the smaller guy could react, Brady jabbed him in the eye with the tip of his cue, leaving a swath of blue chalk across his cheek. In the three seconds it took Brady to hit the door, he couldn't resist yelling, "I'm not a fucking Scout, I'm a police officer!"

"You're a hothead," Brady's captain explained later as he pushed the mandatory resignation papers across his desk. "We don't need your type on the force."

Funny because, as far as Brady could tell, the force was full of his type. Ironically, the bar fight didn't cost Brady his job. Wearing his uniform off-duty and announcing that he was a cop did. A firing offense, had he read the fine print. The first of many dreams shattered.

That was 1985, the year Brady drifted down to Laughlin for the first time, hot on the trail of a minimum-wage security guard gig at the Riverside. After getting bounced from the academy and the ensuing breakup with Jennifer, his high school sweetheart, he heeded the siren call of the late-night commercials for Holiday Shores, a bedroom community just across the Colorado River from Laughlin. Don Adams (not the Don Adams of "Get Smart" fame but a fat, balding pitchman), touted the cheap riverfront lots, close to "schools, churches, shopping, recreation."

Also close to double-wides, bait-and-tackle shops, and meth labs. Brady didn't care. He fit right into this makeshift town of losers running away from their fucked-up lives. He made the move on an August day with the mercury topping out at 121, the sweat pouring off him in torrents, making little explosions in the dust. He moved his meager belongings into a 400-square-foot efficiency unit on Ramar Road, the kind with the living room and bedroom separated by a half-wall with a swivel TV bolted to the top. The refrigerator was just big enough for a couple of Hungry Man dinners and a sixer of Bud.

He met Shari, his future ex-wife, at the piano bar of the tiny Regency Casino, so small it was like hanging out in someone's living room, listening to old bluesman Jimmy Beasley paying tribute to even older bluesmen like Muddy Waters and Howlin' Wolf. Afterward, he took her to the Regency's restaurant for the $2.95 prime rib special, then took her home to bed.

They shared a love for the blues, the smell of the river, and early-morning sex. Brady thought it would be enough. They got married three months later at American Legion Post 87 with a Cold Duck and Cheese Whiz reception for anyone hanging around the bar. An overnight honeymoon in Lake Havasu at a motel with a number in the name sealed the deal.

A week later, they were already bickering about his gambling, her drinking. Then *his* drinking. Brady stuck it out three more years, just to convince himself he gave it his best shot. When he found that he enjoyed flushing the toilet while she showered just to hear her scream, he knew it was time to get the hell out.

Brady never did buy that riverfront lot. Too bad. It would have been worth almost $200,000 today. Enough to retire down in Baja like his friend George. Instead, he invested his money at the Riverside craps tables, management being only too happy to recoup its wages before Brady could even exit the building.

By 1987, the gravitational pull of Las Vegas proved too strong and sucked Brady back into its orbit, not an unusual occurrence. Ex-pats often returned, although they could rarely explain why. He bounced around from job to job, woman to woman. Landed at Gaming Control for a while. Never missed Laughlin, never had reason to go back. Until now.

Thirty miles after Searchlight, Brady turned left onto 163 and began the twenty-five-mile descent into that massive bowl of rock, the heat already radiating upward in shimmering waves. Cotton candy clouds hung low on the horizon, picking up moisture from the river. Turning gray, like Brady's mood. He steered the old Ford past the Mojave Generating Station where his neighbor, Pedro, had melted in a boiler explosion years before. Past Davis Dam, a quick right onto Casino Drive, also known as the Laughlin Strip, a low-rent Vegas wannabe, its tall, white towers standing guard on both sides of the roadway.

He continued past a mobile home park, casino lots crammed with enough motorcycles to put a Harley dealership to shame, past familiar names like the Tropicana and Golden Nugget and Flamingo, looking nothing like their more famous Vegas brethren, their marquees trumpeting George Thorogood, Vince Gill, and Davey Jones, to target Laughlin's triple demographic of bikers, rednecks, and old folks. Past the miniature Regency Casino, faded and peeling, now dwarfed by high-rises. He felt a kinship with the place. Two dinosaurs, somehow still standing. It was the only thing he recognized, other than the river itself.

* * *

"People say I'm arrogant. Self-centered. A sociopath, even. . ."

Jeremy "Germy" Boozer, a fat, greasy coil of black hair and nervous energy, prowled the small stage of Sammy's Comedy by the Shore, a 250-seat club tucked away in the ass-end of the island-themed River Palms Casino.

"I'm here to tell you, I've seen the error of my ways. This is the first time I've said this in public." Long pause. "I have embraced Jesus Christ as my personal Lord and Savior."

A low murmur from the sparse two-for-one crowd taking in the afternoon show as a respite from the heat and gambling. Not exactly the sort of material you'd expect in a joint like this, Brady thought as he nursed a Diet Coke and lemon from the anonymity of his table near the rear exit.

"I know now that Jesus Christ died for my sins." Another pause. "But only for *my* sins. The rest of you dipshits are on your own."

From somewhere near the stage, a beer bottle whizzed past

Boozer's head, splattering against a fake palm tree. A dumpy middle-aged couple wearing identical yellow "Colorado River Rat" T-shirts stood up and waddled toward the door, muttering something about "sacrilege." A whiskey-soaked voice screamed, "You're going to hell!" As the man behind the voice rushed the stage, two security guards wrestled him to the floor.

"Thank you!" Boozer yelled in response. "You've been a great audience. I'll be here 'til Tuesday."

Not bloody likely, Brady thought. But he knew Boozer had the dirt on everybody. It was how he kept his gigs. Precisely the reason why Brady figured this was as good a place as any to start his investigation. Brady may have been the only human on Earth who actually liked the fat fuck. He was just the kind of asshole he usually got along with.

The comic bounded from the stage and made his way through the maze of tables and chairs, stopping briefly to down a half-empty glass of beer abandoned by one of the previous patrons, wiping his mouth with the back of his hairy hand.

"Germy, over here!" Brady shouted at the big man. Boozer flinched, an automatic response, before focusing his eyes on Brady.

"Danny boy!" Boozer said as the two men shook hands warmly. "What's it been, three, four years?"

"More like five," Brady said. "You're looking well. Other than that shiner."

Indeed, Boozer did look well. He was one of those guys who hit the wall early and stayed there. It coincided with Brady's theory that ugly people age better. Not giving a shit about anything helped, too.

"Can I buy you a beer?"

"Stupid question," Boozer grinned. "Make it two."

"I see you haven't changed the act much," Brady said as the server set down their drinks.

"I like to elicit an emotional response. You know that."

"That's what you call it now? Pissing people off?"

"It's what I do best. Performance art." Boozer picked up his Miller Light and took a giant swig. "Like Kaufman. Kinison. All the way back to Kovacs. You know what those guys had in common?"

"Last names starting with K?"

Boozer shook his head slowly. "All dead. Car crash. Lung cancer. Car crash. Kinison bought it on Highway 95, just outside Needles. Can you believe it? Genius like that dies in fucking Needles. Now there's a joke for you."

"The way of the world," Brady said.

"Amen, brother. On a happier note, you should have been here last night. Audience was mainly African-American. Some kind of Southern Baptist convention. So I trotted out the Stevie Wonder material. You remember that, right?"

Brady remembered how that material almost got Boozer killed.

"You didn't," was all he could say.

"Yep. Asked if anyone had seen the Grammys. Why the hell do they always stick Stevie Wonder in the front row? What a waste of a good seat."

"Don't tell me, that's how you got the black eye."

"Couple guys jumped me in the parking lot. Security broke it up. Although I think they waited just a little too long, if you know what I mean."

Brady knew. A lot of people wouldn't mind watching Boozer get the snot beat out of him.

"You're a brave man, Germy. Or stupid. I'm not sure which." He raised his glass in mock salute.

Boozer gave a little bow. "I take both as a compliment." Then, turning serious. "I know you didn't come all this way just to shoot the shit. That's some story you told me on the phone. What the hell have you gotten yourself into this time?"

Brady swirled the ice around in his glass, raised it to his lips, thought better of it. His stomach was doing back flips. Jesus, it was getting to where the only things he could keep down were club soda and saltines. "That's what I'm trying to find out. What've you heard on the street?"

"Not much. Rumors. Hearsay. Innuendo. Hey, not a bad title for my next comedy album."

"Which would also be your *first* comedy album." Without thinking, Brady sipped his Coke and winced. At least the dim light in here made his head feel a little better.

"But seriously, folks, a buddy of mine works the cage at the Aquarius, says he's heard rumblings about some kind of money-laundering scheme, a crew from up your way."

Brady leaned in. "Say how much?"

"Dunno. Three hundred, four hundred K. That neighborhood. A lot of dough for our little neck of the desert."

"This buddy of yours got a name?"

"Yeah, but he won't talk to you. Or anyone, for that matter. He's skittish.

"There's something else, too. Bogus twenties started showing up on the river last month. Treasury was down here for a few days, but they came up empty. Except for the funny money they confiscated from my tip jar."

"Unbelievable," Brady said. "Somebody left you a tip."

Boozer let loose a booming guffaw. "You should write comedy. Come see me if the bottom falls out of the P.I. biz."

"Too late."

"So that's that. Sorry I can't be more helpful. Listen, I got comps for the buffet. Not bad if you stay away from the Salisbury steak. Buy you dinner for old-time sake?"

"Then you'd only owe me ninety-nine more."

He shrugged. "Gotta start somewhere."

"Let me take a rain check. Got a few more things I need to do. You've been a big help."

Boozer's face lit up. "Really? Nobody ever said that to me before."

* * *

Brady spent the rest of the day wandering around Laughlin, hoping to overhear a snippet of useful conversation, making himself just visible enough to attract the attention of Gravel Voice if that was part of the plan. From time to time, he'd sneak a peek to see if he was being followed. But if he had a tail, the guy knew what he was doing. At the pink-windowed but otherwise generic Aquarius Casino, he wasted a few quarters in the "Invaders from the Planet Moolah" slots, then bought into a low-limit seven-card stud game. Amazing the things you can hear at a poker table. A hundred forty dollars later (and lighter), all he knew for sure was that the Davey Jones show blew and some old duffer's wife picked up a nasty case of food poisoning at an Italian place across the river. Had it all been a waste of time? Brady was starting to think someone just wanted him out of the way for a while. But why?

Late in the afternoon, he drove across the bridge into Bullhead City and made a couple of passes through town, now practically unrecognizable, the mom-and-pops replaced by Wal-Mart and Lowe's. True what they say, you can't go home again. Assuming this was ever home in the first place. On his last go-round, he spied Valdo's Mexican Restaurant, a solitary holdover from the past. Brady's mood brightened. The chili Colorado was as good as he remembered.

* * *

The angry flashing lights just before Searchlight caught Brady by surprise. He had been obeying the speed limit, as far as he could tell with the odometer disconnected. Knowing the drill, he dug through the glove box for proof of insurance and registration (still no list), rolled down his window, and kept his hands in plain sight at ten and two on the steering wheel. A glimpse in the rearview mirror revealed three units. Odd. Maybe they were just bored, nothing much to do in this armpit town. Another glance showed the cruisers to be Metro Crown Vics, not NHP. As Brady pondered his predicament, a no-nonsense voice barked through the PA, "Driver, let me see your hands!"

Brady's mouth went dry as he followed the order.

Then, "Driver, turn the vehicle off with your left hand!"

Then, "Driver, open the door from the outside with your left hand!"

Then, "Driver, step out of the car with your hands in the air!"

Bile and salsa burned the back of his throat.

"Driver, walk backwards to the sound of my voice. Stop! Go down to your knees!"

Brady did as he was told.

The voice, much closer now. "On your stomach. Leave your arms flat out to your sides. Cross your legs at the ankles and bring your feet up to your buttocks."

A pair of sandpaper paws trussed Brady like a rodeo calf. Lying in the gravel and dust, his shoulder blades already howling in protest, Brady raised his eyes just enough to see an officer pop open his trunk. The dangling lifeless hand with the bright red nail polish and delicate Chinese tattoo looked all too familiar.

Lil.

Chapter Four

BY LEAH BAILLY

There were so many ways this could end.

Clamped into cuffs on the side of a forsaken highway, the officer's knee in his back, his cheek ground into the searing asphalt, wrists wrenched behind him — Brady listed the options, reeling them off one by one:

The electric chair. Lethal injection. Thirty squandered years in a cell in Ely, some bruiser's cocoa-puff or a guard's little pet. After all, a lady cop was found dead in his trunk, and the officers shouting his name and details into their radios didn't seem to think it was coincidental, accidental, unfair.

"Suspect has been detained! I repeat! We have the suspect here!"

A helicopter could swoop down from the sky, a spray of bullets miraculously murdering each of the officers, reducing the three squad cars to flat tires and pierced shells, their radios silenced, the handcuffs knocked from Brady's wrists.

"White, middle-aged male. I repeat, requesting back-up!"

Maybe Lil could suddenly come alive! Maybe she wasn't dead at all, just drugged into a stupor from which she could magically awaken and explain the entire thing to these six khakied officers, who'd then release Brady and allow him to walk free. Little tears leaked from Brady's eyes.

"Maybe she's alive —" Brady managed. But the knee dug deeper into his spine.

"Shut the fuck up, asshole." The officer's gun prodded the back of Brady's neck.

More tears. More terrible options. He could be hanged. Tortured for information that he did not have. He could point the finger at Samuels, at Tommy, at anyone with any connection to this nice-looking policewoman, impossibly dead and stuffed into his trunk. He could choke himself right here on the side of the road to avoid the punishment. Brady held his breath, hoping to pass out, but failed, gasping after thirty seconds. The gun jabbed against his skull. Brady wished it would go off.

"Awaiting orders! Sir. I repeat. We have the suspect here."

He could confess even though he hadn't done anything, never killed a man, or woman, in his entire career. It would get him off the pavement at least, get this brute's knee off his back to let a little more air into his lungs. Or he could act like a crazy person, drooling and wailing and pleading insanity. If he started early enough, maybe they would believe him.

"Sir, could you repeat the order? What the —"

Or the Christian Bikers! Jesus could look down from his little kingdom in heaven and tip off the Blue Diamond Gang and they'd all charge up on their Harleys and politely kick the shit out of these officers and they'd lift him up and onto the back of Axel's ride and they'd charge up the highway back to Vegas. It would buy him a couple of hours, enough time to prove his innocence. Enough time to shove that fourteen grand down Samuels' throat for getting him into this mess. Maybe shove a pistol in *his* neck.

"You lucky little fucker! You lucky little —"

Of all the possible permutations and combinations, of the thousands of escape plans or suicide attempts or motion picture moves that could have released him from this horrible, fatal, impossible situation, the last one he expected was this:

The knee lifted off Brady's back.

Painlessly.

Then the gun disappeared. With it, the cuffs. And with the cuffs, the officer.

With the disappearance of the officer came the sound of engines starting, of gravel crunching, and of tires squealing away. And with the disappearance of the three squad cars, the body. Brady looked up from his position, face-down on the road, and all he saw was his empty trunk. Lil's deflated, deceased little body had disappeared. Vanished. All in a matter of seconds.

And with the disappearing squad cars, the officers, the dead body in his trunk, Brady nearly lost his hold on his consciousness. He nearly passed out, but stopped himself, forced his eyes open. Forced air into his lungs. Struggling at first, Brady made his way to his feet. In the distance he saw the disappearing squad cars, all returning south, back to Searchlight, from where they came.

He steadied himself against his tires, then shuffled to the passenger side, gulping air.

The door was flung open. He sat for a second, then remembered to look for things. His wallet: gone. His cell phone: gone. The fourteen thousand dollars: missing. Of course.

His face aching, those few bits of gravel still lodged into the flesh of his cheek, Brady brushed his stubble with the back of his hand. They had left him like that, only the keys in the ignition. He rubbed the flesh of his wrists and still gasping, dropped his head between his knees.

A car passed. Then slowed. Then stopped.

Brady shook his head. Willing the car to keep moving, but it did not.

The car was black. A Mercedes. Brady slammed his door closed, then reached across to the driver's-side door and yanked it too, kicking his legs over the stick shift and clumsily climbing into the driver's seat, trying to start the car and drive somewhere, anywhere, immediately, now.

But the car blocked his path. A man in a black suit popped open his door and approached Brady, a giant magnum pointed at Brady's face. He motioned for him to unlock the door, which he did, his vision blurring, his breath catching in his throat. And when the gun was pointed at his temple, as he lifted himself from the driver's seat and back out onto the highway, Brady expected to die, right there, a few miles outside Searchlight, all for fourteen thousand measly dollars and a murder case gone sour.

The man in the black suit didn't even need to swipe the magnum across Brady's jaw. Without any effort from the suited man, Brady crumpled, a worthless heap at the man's feet.

* * *

It felt like mid-afternoon, and Brady was lying on top of the covers on a bed in a hotel room he did not recognize. The air was cooled and smelled sort of stylish, the mixture of far-away casino, cologne and leather couch. He could make out a red-felt pool table at the far end of an adjoining room; an ensuite bathroom glimmered to his left, the lights above the vanity, dimmed.

Brady was back in Las Vegas, he was sure, because no place in Laughlin or Searchlight or Needles would have a wet bar built into the suite, or one-inch Italian tile, or vased lilies, or even real leather on the couches. Sun was coming in thick between red curtains. The phone worked.

His tongue was dry and swollen, like his mouth had been open a while, but he wouldn't drink the water beside the bed, moving to the wet bar instead, and after several mouthfuls from the tap and a splash on his face, he heard the cue ball on the pool table make that unmistakable crack. He froze. The figure of a girl passed in front of the door.

She was in a white dress with a gold bikini strap underneath and wore her tanned legs very well under it all. They were long; Brady noticed right away, about the same moment he realized she could not have been older than twenty-one. Music tinkled in the suite's main room, and she was humming along. There didn't seem to be anyone else at the table with her. Brady ran his fingers through his hair, making sure he hadn't been hit in the head; his skull was intact. He steadied his feet under him and took a few steps toward the doorway. She looked relieved.

"What the fuck."

"Hello," Brady said. He braced himself against the door's frame and leaned into the room, checking the back couches, the second water bar. The flat-screen flashed from the far wall. The glass table was bare.

"I was totally scared you were, like, dead."

Brady looked harder at the girl, and noticed that she wasn't as young close up as she had appeared from across the room. Heavy mascara and dark eyebrows seemed to crease up her eyes. Not a natural blonde. "Nobody killed me this time. Thirsty, though."

"They'll be right back, they're getting drinks."

"Who?"

"You could use a drink, I bet."

"Who's coming?"

The girl coughed. "I called your cell phone twice. Do you recognize my voice?"

The music got louder. Brady scanned the countertop for anything that could have belonged to him. The girl breezed closer. She smelled like the lilies.

"Your friends have my wallet," Brady said.

The girl reached out a hand to Brady's forearm and he stepped back, leaving his arm under her touch. "Listen. Axel and Ilene are missing." Brady looked at the girl again; her skin was red, tender in spots, like she had spent too much time outside in the Vegas afternoons. She brushed her hair out of her eyelashes. "I called you about it before."

"And you are —"

"We need your help, to get Axel back. And Ilene."

"You're the sister." Brady moved behind the bar and called his own phone, then let it go to voicemail. He hung up without checking his messages. Then dialed again from the second bedroom. There was no imprint on the second duvet, the bed untouched.

"They're in shit," the girl hollered from the other room. "The nurse said she checked out early, and Axel never called." She pursed her lips at Brady from the doorway of the bedroom. "Now it's just me. All . . . alone."

Brady rolled his eyes and brushed the curtains aside. There was one message, from this girl, Ilene's sister and granddaughter of the deceased. "I really gotta talk to you, Mr. Brady. My name is Juliet." She sounded like such a little kid on the phone, her voice nervous and infantile compared with the woman's in the next room. He hung up.

Out the hotel window, the pool below swarmed with bodies. People clumped together, he could make out cabanas and long drinks and a throng of half-submerged bikinis, the pool slick with grease. He had heard about these parties: swim-up black-jack, silicone, and an excuse to spread the latest STDs. Music thumped from giant poolside speakers. He checked the hotel stationery and realized they were in the same hotel as his first meeting with Samuels, just a different suite.

He shuffled back toward the wet bar and poured himself a pint of tap water, his face sore, his neck and shoulders aching from the pistol, the monkey who wrenched his arms into cuffs. He gulped down half the glass, his patience waning. "Listen, Juliet," he muttered. The girl's mouth opened a little, lips glossed.

Brady slammed his empty glass down on the marble. "How the fuck did I get here?"

"Wait!" The girl's face went white. Across the room, the little green light above the doorknob clicked on. The handle moved.

Brady reached for the counter, his vision suddenly swimming.

The door swung open. "Ah! Mr. Daniel Brady." Quinton Samuels strolled across the carpet in chinos and loafers, no socks. His silver hair was carefully brushed back, his shirt unbuttoned around the throat. Creepy Kevin followed carrying two briefcases, allowing the door to click shut behind him. "I see you've awakened. That wasn't an easy situation to get you out of, Mr. Brady. I expect you are quite grateful."

"I . . . I would have been okay." Brady's voice felt raw.

"Please, after these events, I'm quite sure you could take a cocktail."

Brady nearly gagged. Kevin poured a long gin and tonic for Samuels, but Brady declined. "What the hell happened out there? What happened to my friend Lillian?"

"We've . . . we're working on that, Mr. Brady"

"But is she alive? She's . . ."

"We can't answer that yet."

"God," Juliet whispered, suddenly tucked behind Brady.

"I see you've met Colleen's granddaughter. Now tell me, what did you come up with in Laughlin?"

"Not much." Brady sunk to the couch. Juliet nestled in next to him. The combined smell of the girl and Samuels' gin made Brady's mouth water.

"You didn't speak to anyone? You have nothing?" Samuels moved to the window to take in the scene from the pool party below. He shook his head.

Brady wiped his mouth. "A counterfeit crew whose work is leaking south. Waste of time, I think. It was like somebody wanted me out of Vegas for a minute." Brady stood and looked at Kevin, square. "Where did they take her?"

"Who's they, Mr. Brady?" Samuels called from the window.

"You tell me."

Samuels sighed and took a long drink. "It's a lot of money they've stolen from me, Mr. Brady. This so-called crew. I'm afraid our sweet, deceased Colleen was in on their little scam, the jackpots, using fake bills. I'm still in need of a good private detective."

"What the hell."

"It was my capital involved, Mr. Brady. You understand. Losing Colleen was like losing a considerable investment. With her death, the funds have disappeared."

"Look. This's got nothing to do with me." Brady pushed himself toward the door.

"Wait. You need these." Samuels motioned to Kevin, who

passed Brady a metal dish holding his phone, wallet, and keys. The wallet had all of his cards, no cash. "I'll double the initial payment when you find Ilene and Axel." Samuels handed Brady another small envelope.

"What about Lil?"

"We'll follow up on that."

"What about the girl?"

Juliet stood. "I'm right here. Don't speak to me like I'm not right —"

"You're taking her with you." Brady glanced at Juliet, her pouting mouth, her blank eyes. "You'll need a driver."

"What, you don't trust me?" The girl winked at Brady, then drifted toward the door, and just as she did, the green light clicked on again, and the handle turned. Brady was shoving his wallet and phone into his pocket when two men entered the room, dressed in identical dark suits, bulging at the hip. The music paused. Brady nearly choked. The first man he recognized from the highway rescue, the man who must have collected him off the smoldering asphalt and escorted him back to Vegas. But the second man was the kicker. Tommy. The faux bartender. They locked eyes as Brady brushed past him, following the girl out into the shadowy hall.

* * *

The cherry convertible swept across the freeway, so fast that

Brady had to brace himself against the dash. Between his feet, Juliet's gold lamé purse started to jingle, and she reached for it, ignoring the road.

"Jesus!" Brady shouted, and she returned her gaze to the highway. It was sunset against the backside of the Strip, with all that perfect sun and the wind rushing around them, the FM on loud.

"I love this town!" Juliet shouted into the turquoise sky. She clenched her pink fingernails against the wheel and tossed her head back. "Love! Love!"

"Watch it," Brady muttered. But she was right about one thing. It was Sin City's magic hour, the billboard light spilling onto the traffic, everything painted gold by the sunset, the palm trees along the exit ramp, shivering.

"We'll go to our place, me and Ilene's. You'll get clues!" Juliet checked her pink mouth in the visor mirror as Brady sunk lower into the leather seat.

"This is bullshit."

"What?" she yelled.

"I got Lil into this. And Axel, I mean, it was me who went to him for the names. And your grandma is dead and your sister is missing." He looked at Juliet, but her mouth was moving to the words of the pop song, ignoring him. "We gotta call the police station," he said louder.

"What?"

"What the hell is wrong with you?!" Brady nearly shouted it in her face. Juliet turned the FM down and glared at the exit signs, annoyed. Brady wouldn't relent. "You're happy now? You act like this is good news, your sister missing."

"Shut up." Juliet set her jaw.

"What are you getting out of all this, huh? What is he paying you?"

Juliet looked over at him, then lifted her sunglasses to the crown of her head. "I told you to shut up," she hissed. The car drifted nearly off the freeway and somebody honked from the opposite lane.

"So your sister's out of the picture and you get work."

Juliet snapped. "Fuck you."

She was probably a pro, Brady thought, and any work was better than that. The Skin City scene was grotesque, raunchy. Brady pictured pretty Juliet, or Ilene, sprawled across a blackjack table in a teddy and thong and Gucci perfume and nothing else. Under her seething body, there would be chips, hundreds of them, each worth more than her weekly check. He pictured a guy like Samuels seated at the table, raising the champagne flute to her mouth and making her sip. The dealer laying cards across her torso, the teddy raised — one face down, one face up — Samuels' brushing the cards across her breasts. Hit me, he'd whisper. Hit me again.

Brady shuddered.

The car veered right onto the exit ramp and deep into East Charleston. Boulder Highway. Sketchville. Land of kitchenettes and weekly rentals and massage parlors with cheap boob-job quacks in the back. The sun was down completely by the time Juliet pulled up to a three-story motel, iron balcony and half-flashing sign. A heavy-gutted thug in a wife-beater and sweatpants eyed the convertible from the office doorway as they stepped out onto the street, the pavement still warm.

"Lookie lookie," he called down to Juliet, who ignored him.

"We left Henderson last year. Foreclosed on our condo." Juliet tried to grin. "But this was closer to work anyways." Outside of apartment number 211, she pulled a key from her gold purse, and then shoved the door with her hip before she pushed through. "Home sweet home!" she trilled.

The fluorescent overhead buzzed on. The room was disgusting. Inside-out underwear and dresses littered the threadbare carpet; half-drunk Coronas and bottles of cheap perfume lined the window sill. The smell of pot overwhelmed him, stale pot, mixed with stale beer and stale bodies. There was a microwave and a hotplate at the far end of the room, past the two double beds, beside a sink overflowing with crusted take-out containers and crumpled-up fast food bags. There was a purse there too, a pink one, half-open. Brady picked his way across the room toward it, kicking the dresses aside. Then he stopped. Heard something. A bump from the bathroom. Juliet breathed in.

"Shit."

The door to the bathroom was slightly ajar, and through the crack Brady could make out a male figure, medium build, his face hiding behind the open medicine cabinet. Brady narrowed his eyes and reached for an emptied beer bottle. He looked at Juliet for a nod, a knowing look, but she was back to her blank, pale self. Brady's grip tightened around the bottle. His neck, throbbing.

"What the fuck!" Brady smashed the butt of the bottle against the doorframe and the man jumped. Screamed. Threw his hands up, spewing pills over the bathroom floor. He was a lanky Asian male, early thirties, with impeccable clothing, Brady noticed right away. He lowered his hands.

"Ohhh, shit!" the man groaned at Brady. "What are *you* doing here?"

Brady dropped the bottle slightly and the man shoved past Brady out of the bathroom toward Juliet.

"We're looking for clues." Juliet looked at him, lip quivering.

"Oh for Christ's sake, girl. Does Samuels know you're here?" The man spoke with a surprising Oklahoma City drawl and wide gestures. He reached for Juliet's purse but she jerked it away.

"He sent me here! What are you doing here?" Juliet yelped.

"Who is this?" Brady stepped toward them, the bottle limp in his hand.

"Oh, this is rich." The man closed his eyes and reached past Juliet for a pack of Marlboros half-open on the sill. He lit one with a deft flick of a Zippo, blowing smoke in Juliet's face. "You didn't see that I just called you?"

"Who the fuck is this?" Brady shouted. His hand was aching from the blow to the bottle. His face burned. "Answer me!" Brady hissed. But both of them just looked stunned.

So he lost it. Enough with this lying girl, the millionaire with his easy money. His missing friends. Brady lunged for Juliet and gripped her around the throat, held the bottle to her neck. The girl whimpered. The room seemed to shrink around him. Brady looked straight at the man, edging the glass toward her skin, and wheezed, "You got five seconds to tell me who you are."

The man shrugged and pursed his mouth. His shoulders bristled. He took a drag from his Marlboro, and breathed it out his nose. "You want to know? Fine. I'm the Creamer."

"Who?"

The girl moaned.

"Yeah. Mr. Creamer. I'm the lawyer."

"The what?" Brady tightened his grip around the girl's neck, whose mouth was suddenly agape, eyes wide.

"The lawyer," Creamer smirked. "The one who's pulling this whole goddamned thing together." The man flicked his ash onto the carpet between his feet, dusting a feather boa, then kicked it lightly with the toe of his shoe. Outside, an engine backfired, and somebody hollered. The girl whined and the Creamer sighed, suddenly exhausted. "Let her go. You happy now? I told you I'm the lawyer. I'm in charge."

"In charge of what?"

"Don't!" Juliet screamed and Brady pressed the glass to her skin. It felt good. He dug a little deeper.

"The set-up!" the Creamer shouted. "The set-up. Fuck! Let her fucking go!"

Disgusted, Brady shoved Juliet away from him, and she stumbled toward the Creamer's arms. He kissed her lightly on the forehead as she crumpled onto the bed. Brady dropped the broken bottle onto a little pile of pantyhose and slumped down beside it.

"A set-up," Brady mumbled.

"You shouldn't have told him." Juliet looked at Brady for the first time with a flicker of disdain, almost pity in her green eyes. Not the best actress, but better looking now that she had melted into her real self. Brady reached for his phone, but didn't have anyone to call. Juliet started to sniffle. "'Cause now we got real fucking problems."

The Creamer flicked his ash at Brady's feet. The dull evening heat pushed in through the open door, mingling with the rotten smell of garbage, melted tar, far-away grease from some dingy Boulder Highway diner.

"Jesus," Brady mumbled, and motioned to the Creamer for

a cigarette.

"Nobody was supposed to die," Juliet muffled into the Creamer's shoulder, and the Creamer shrugged and pulled her closer.

"Lillian," Brady said. Juliet nodded and wailed a little, and Brady pointed a finger at the Creamer. "You and Samuels and Tommy," Brady raised his eyebrows, then saw his shaky hand between them. His voice dropped. "You were after Lil from the beginning."

Juliet let out a little sob.

Creamer stroked Juliet's hair. "Baby, you just calm down. Brady here works for us too. We're like a big family." Juliet looked up at the Creamer with her pretty green eyes, that mascara swiped all down her cheeks. "And if Brady here wants to know who killed his girlfriend, he's gonna stick around."

Brady shuddered again, almost cold. The Creamer leaned toward Brady and clicked open the lighter, and even though he didn't want it, Brady took in a gulp of smoke. Out on the highway, a siren tore through the hot air and the lights from downtown twinkled through the curtains.

Brady picked up a child's doll from the sheets, then tossed it back on a pillow. "What kind of nutjob millionaire would set this all up?" he muttered. But neither one of them would answer, so Brady just stared out the smudged window over the little diners and taco joints and slum hotels, all the way to the lights of the Strip, sparkling despite it all.

Chapter Five

BY JOHN L. SMITH

B rady looked around the room. Suddenly everything was becoming clear. Why hadn't he noticed it sooner? He'd seen rooms like this on occasion during his days as a Gaming Control Board agent.

A seething anger boiled inside him, but for the moment he measured his breathing. The room was far filthier than its occupants. Creamer the lawyer hadn't been there long.

Juliet didn't fit the place, either. Her makeup was too perfect. Not the heavy slap most dancers use out of habit, but the kind of detail around the eyes and cheekbones that takes time. She also was wearing a wig to make her look like more like the photo of Ilene.

Most of all, her emotions didn't fit the moment. It was a dead tell.

"I need to get some air," Brady said, making no eye contact and palming Juliet's car keys.

In two minutes Brady was pulling into a 7-Eleven and dropping a quarter into the pay phone. The recorded voice operator from NV Energy came on the line. He punched in a four-digit code.

"This is Roy Harris."

"It's Brady."

"Hey, brother. What's happening? I'm about to head home for the night."

"Everything in a hurry. I'll tell you about it when I can. Right now I need some help. I need the turn-on date and background on two apartments." He read the addresses to his friend, a twenty-five-year power company employee.

"When do you need it?"

"Yesterday."

"I'll see what I can do. Everything all right?"

"Getting punked and not liking it. I'll call you. Don't use my cell today."

"I'm on it."

"Thanks."

Another quarter, another number.

"Sonny's Southside."

"Dominic. It's Brady."

"My man. Long time no see."

"I don't hang in the bars much anymore."

"You could stop by a friend's place for a cup of coffee once in a while. We got a dayside bartender so sweet she makes the old men cry in their beer."

"I'll take you up on it sometime. But now I need something."

"Name it, baby. I owe you big, you know that. Since you caught those stringers who were robbing me blind, business is good even with that fucking smoking ban. Imagine, a smoking ban in Vegas bars. Figlio di puttana."

"Knowing you, you don't pay too much attention to that one."

"Yeah, not too much. We keep an eye out for FBI agents with smoke detectors."

"Your cousin. You know, the one with the auto fetish?"

Silence on the line as Dominic registered the message. Brady would never mention his cousin, Little Vic Paduano, on any phone line. Little Vic was a connected guy who owned chop shops from Las Vegas to Mexicali.

"I don't see him much," Dominic said.

"I know you don't. But I have a donation for him. It's a beater. I can't fix it. It's got some kind of bug that's beyond me. He can have it. What I want is for him to show me the problem and give me his expert opinion before he Siegfried & Roys it. It's got to be done very quickly. I'll leave the keys in it at the 7-Eleven at 3051 E. Charleston."

"I'll take care of it, baby. Hang tight."

* * *

This far out on the east end of Las Vegas it's useless to call for a cab. They're focused on hustling customers up and down the Strip, out to McCarran Airport, and over to the string of topless bars that pay kickbacks to drivers to deliver hopelessly horny marks wearing monogrammed sports shirts and too much cologne.

But in a tough economy there's always someone willing to give a guy a ride, especially when there's quick money in it. Brady stopped a construction worker coming out of the convenience store with a six-pack of Budweiser. The guy's hair was full of dust. He had the coyote eyes of a meth tweaker. His T-shirt had sweat rings on its sweat rings. Even his bulging pitbull forearm tats looked tired. He wore the heavy boots of a laborer and looked up from them when Brady explained that he needed a ride across town. When Brady flashed a C-note, the laborer grinned, his rotted yellow teeth catching the artificial light.

For two hundred more dollars, the laborer agreed to trade his scuffed cell phone for Brady's new one, neglecting to inform his newfound benefactor that it was a Wal-Mart throw-down with limited minutes.

Brady hated to lose his new phone, but he couldn't take chances on someone tracking him. He was feeling a little paranoid, but then he was the one being set up for a heavy fall.

"You in some kind of trouble?" yellow teeth asked, drinking a beer and driving one-handed.

"Not much," Brady replied.

"Trying to lose the old lady, huh? Yeah, man, I know that feeling," he said. "You got any more of those Benjamins I can hook you up with a piece. Not much for looks, but it shoots good. Five hundred."

"How about two?"

"How about three?"

Brady nodded.

Racing up Tropicana in the left lane, running lights not as yellow as his teeth, the laborer sipped his Budweiser, lit a Marlboro, broke wind, spat out the open window, cursed a Hispanic family in a too-slow Hyundai, and still managed to reach under the seat and pull up an object wrapped in a red mechanic's rag. He handed it to Brady.

"See what you think."

It was a .32 Smith and Wesson with the barrel serial number clumsily filed off. Cloth tape around the handle to cut down on print transfer. No doubt hot as a skillet. From its heft, Brady knew it was loaded.

He peeled off three bills from his bankroll and said, "You can drop me off at the next corner."

The tweaker nodded and sealed the deal with a lugee out the window.

* * *

Back at his apartment complex, Brady knocked on the door of his neighbor, Helen McGreevey. She was eighty, had worked at the original El Rancho Vegas for Belden Katleman in the early '50s. She broke in as an underage shill at the El Cortez when Benny Siegel took over the race wire there. At the El Rancho, she fell in love with Irish Charlie McGreevey, a skilled casino man killed by Johnny Marshall, who was of course never prosecuted for the crime. Helen was known as the first female floorman in Las Vegas. She was tougher than Tyson on cheaters and would point out card counters by ridiculing their arithmetic. "What are you, counting with your fingers and toes?" she'd roar in her cigarette-scarred voice for everyone in the blackjack pit to hear.

Helen's eyesight was nearly gone, but she heard everything. She answered Brady's knock with "I wondered when you'd come to your senses and start courting an old broad."

Brady had to laugh. Before he could respond, she said, "But don't start trying to charm me at this late date. I know what you want. You want to know if you've had any recent visitors, and the answer is yes. Two fellows claiming to be from the telephone company were at your door this morning. And they entered your apartment."

"Thanks, Helen," Brady said. "I think I need a favor."

"I thought you'd never ask."

She welcomed him in and returned a moment later with a set of car keys.

"I haven't driven the Cadillac since my last eye surgery, but I start it regularly and play the radio and pretend I'm going out on the town. Oh, this place used to be so glamorous. It was really something when the mob ran it. Except for that nasty bastard Johnny Marshall, may his soul burn in hell."

Brady had heard the story of her husband's violent death many times, but he listened patiently. Then he borrowed the old woman's phone, leaving a hundred-dollar bill on the kitchen counter where even a nearly blind woman would find it.

"What do you have for me?" Brady asked his power company pal Roy Harris.

"You're lucky. The Budget Hacienda Apartments rent by the month. And it's not two apartments they've got, but three. Leased for six months to Desert Mirage Productions. Power was turned on four weeks ago. One apartment uses almost no electricity. The other two use more."

Brady thanked his friend, assured him they'd get together soon. After thanking Helen McGreevey for her assistance, he dashed across the hall to his apartment and unlocked the door quickly, the .32 in his pocket. The blinking light of his message phone pierced the shadow: two calls.

Call one:

"Brady. It's Smith. Call me, man. I have something hot for you."

Call two:

"What'd you do with my car, asshole?" a drunk woman's voice snarled. It was the woman who called herself Juliet. "I heard from Ilene. She's in trouble and needs your help. Call Samuels right away. And give me my car back, will you?"

Brady went to his closet and quickly picked up his surveillance bag, which held electronics equipment he used in his P.I. job, and hurried back out the door. In the covered parking area, he started the root beer-colored '85 Eldorado, its interior reeking of cigarettes and the fine dust of neglect and fading memories.

As he was pulling out, a black-and-white with what appeared to be two Metro officers pulled up to the curb. He wrote down its license plate, then watched the blue uniforms go upstairs out of the rearview mirror. Whoever had visited his apartment earlier that day had wired it with a motion detector. And Metro officers wear tan uniforms.

Brady motored back across the valley through the darkness and the overheated traffic. The Cadillac's big V-8 would cost a fortune to run every day, but Brady noticed the twenty-five-year-old yacht had 19,250 miles on it and purred in a double baritone reminiscent of the late Vegas jazz singer Joe Williams.

He made a call from the laborer's cell phone to Dominic "Sonny" Paduano.

"You're a funny guy, Brady, you know that? I love you, baby, but you're a funny guy. That car guy says your jalopy's worth maybe eighty large."

"I've never had extravagant tastes," Brady said.

"It's probably worth another five Gs with all that added-in stuff, he tells me. Very sophisticated. Two cameras, four micro-phones, a GPS tracking system. Everything but Panavision and Cinemascope. My car guy says how much you want for the whole deal?"

"I want the bugging equipment. He can keep the car. He needs to drown the GPS pronto. Tell him he can owe me."

"Done and done," Sonny Paduano said.

On his way over to Sonny's Southside, Brady placed a call to John L. Smith, the *Review-Journal* newspaper columnist.

"Brady?" Smith laughed. "Glad you got the message. Your phone was making crazy noises earlier today. I almost decided you'd gone on a bender and busted out."

"I'm still here; for how much longer is the question."

"Well, you're no doubt feeling better than Fat Andy Sachman. Or should I say Fried Andy. Metro hasn't officially I.D.'d the body, but I've got a back-channel canary who confirms it's Fat

Andy. Body is missing its hands. He must have really pissed somebody off. The body was dumped off State Route 157 three miles up from the highway. 'The Happy Dumping Ground,' as an old Paiute Indian once called it. Anyway, you got a comment for Nevada's largest daily?"

"Tell your readers I'm seeking grief counseling," Brady said, playing his cards carefully with the newspaperman. "Meanwhile, I have a special request. I need everything you can dig up on Joe Don Walker."

"There's a blast from the past. Haven't heard a word from him since he caught that break and got six months of halfway house time on those union corruption charges. He should have been hit with ten years. Instead, he got a wrist slap. What's he up to nowadays?"

"That's what this inquiring mind wants to know."

"I'll float a note in the Friday column. It's better than fishing. And I'll take a look at the clip file. It's been a slow day. Not a single county commissioner has been indicted."

Brady thanked his friend as he was pulling into Sonny's Southside. After an exchange of pleasantries, Brady received a cheese pizza and a paper sack to go. The sack contained a Diet Coke and the pinhole cameras that had been taken out of the actress's car. He was so-so with electronics, but he knew top-of-the-line spyware when he saw it.

The last thing Sonny Paduano had said to him was, "The

GPS is now tracking an eighteen-wheeler somewhere south of Barstow."

One more call to Roy Harris.

"Any chance those apartments can be without power for a couple hours?"

"You don't ask for much, my man."

"It's important."

Harris hesitated.

"It must be," he said.

In thirty minutes, Brady had positioned the Cadillac in the parking lot of the apartment complex. The night swelter was almost unbearable inside the Eldorado. He cracked a window and waited. Somewhere in the night, storm clouds were rolling in.

He watched as the lights went out. In short order, four people came outside. Two lit cigarettes while two others shouted into their cell phones. In a moment, the woman who had been playing Ilene's sister, Juliet, emerged from the apartment, interrupted Creamer the lawyer, and in a moment they locked an apartment and left. An hour later, the sun had finished bleeding behind the Spring Mountains and the night got slightly cooler. Brady waited and fielded a phone call from Harris.

"I'm handling this call personally. It's overtime. But I can't stall it all night. I can give you two hours."

In twenty minutes, Brady's patience paid off. The three men left the other apartments. He grabbed his bag, passed the trashed apartment 211, moved to the second.

In the movies, the private investigator is also a master lock-smith. In reality, a pry bar and a rubber mallet are faster and more effective entry tools. The technique is called peeling a lock. Just place the blade of the bar into the jamb and pound it until the lock breaks or you generate enough leverage to pop the door open. Same for a Kmart dead bolt. Just pound it and peel it. Cheap apartment doors are easier to open than a can of sardines if you don't mind leaving a mess.

Once inside, he saw the glow of three laptop computers run-ning on their batteries. He flipped on his flashlight and saw a small mainframe on rollers in the corner. This was much more upscale than the average porn shoot. There were enough cameras and editing equipment to produce a made-for-TV movie.

He spent the next thirty minutes concealing the pinhole cameras, and another twenty scouring the laptops and collecting disks. When he found the laptop that controlled the pinhole cameras, he closed it and placed it in his bag.

Door No. 3.

The flashlight illuminated a garbage-strewn living room with rented furniture. The bedroom door was closed, and Brady set down his bag and pulled out the .32. Cutting the flashlight, he opened the door slowly, taking care to stay to the side and out of a direct line of fire. Sweat dripped from his forehead and neck.

When he flipped the light back on, "Sonofabitch" was all he could muster.

It was a frail Ilene and the animal, Axel, bound and gagged on a sagging double bed like a reality show version of *Beauty and the Beast*.

After they caught their breath and used the bathroom, Brady told them, "There isn't much time. They'll be coming back soon. You need to keep a very low profile until you hear from me."

"Ain't exactly my style," Axel said, rubbing his wrists.

"Neither is burying your girlfriend here," Brady said.

Brady ushered them out the door and down to the parking lot. Once they were back in the Cadillac and on the road, Brady said, "Get her to a safe place. If you've got cell phones, trash them." He gave them his number, told them to contact him when they were safe, and dropped them at a place on the Boulder Highway that rents dented automobiles cheap to college kids determined to party and drive in Vegas.

Brady still had work to do. It was late when he reached Helen McGreevey's apartment. She was still awake.

"I need a favor, Helen," Brady said.

"Use the spare bedroom," the elderly woman replied.

For the next three hours Brady pored over the disks he'd removed from the apartment. They were copies and mostly unedited material and each was labeled "Eye in the Sky." He saw himself in several of them.

He also saw Fat Andy Sachman, pleading for his life, crying like a baby, and getting shot right in the face before the camera went dark.

He found no sign of Lillian. But there were two scenes featuring Tommy the Binion's bartender in different roles.

And there was a disk devoted to the funeral of Colleen Winters. Ilene Davies was there with Axel at her side. A handful of strangers was present. And Jeremy Boozer, the burned-out comedian who was having trouble keeping a lounge gig in Laughlin.

No Quinton Samuels. He claimed she was his last, lost love, but he didn't bother to attend her funeral.

The images flicked by so quickly that Brady had to reverse the disk several times before capturing the moment. It was an older, grayer and chubbier version of Joe Don Walker, the union thumper. He was seated next to two older men. One Brady recognized as Carl Pistel, the old-school pornographer he was certain would come back as the owner of record of Desert Mirage Productions. The distinguished man next to him was white-haired and impeccably dressed. His face was as slim as a blade. He could have been Gregory Peck's brother.

It was Francis Xavier O'Connor, aide de camp, lifelong friend, and personal spokesman for Nick Nazarian, owner of the second-largest casino company in the world with its flagship, the Desert Paradise. Nazarian is almost ninety. He's the recluse the business writers call "The Ancient Mariner." He's one of a few remaining Nevada gaming licensees whose careers began when Benny Siegel was still building the Flamingo. Bugsy, Gus Greenbaum, Moe Dalitz, Benny Binion, and Kirk Kerkorian. Nazarian had outlived them all. He still golfed every morning, still kept a runway model around his mansion.

Brady said to himself, "When the rich have everything, they will find ways to amuse themselves."

If Nazarian was behind this, it wouldn't end well. He was known to keep sheriffs and former FBI men in his pocket. He was also known as a man who was willing to gamble, but he hated to be cheated.

There was one way to find out whether Nick Nazarian was the man behind the curtain. Get to his assistant, Frankie O'Connor.

Chapter Six

By Constance Ford

B rady lifted his head and looked around, then flopped back down on the maroon and blue Persian rug. Even if old Helen was half-blind, she still knew how to decorate a room. He sat up and rubbed his face. The pattern of the rug was imprinted on his right cheek, as if he'd spent the night lying on a branding iron. He glanced at his watch.

"Damn," he said. Almost noon. He'd fallen asleep eight hours earlier, the laptop still glowing in the darkness, images of Lil and Andy Sachman, Joe Don Walker and Carl Pistel swirling nightmarishly through his brain. Benny Binion, he thought, for the hundredth time. Kirk Kerkorian. Nick Nazarian. Francis Xavier O'Connor. He touched the mouse on the laptop and the list of addresses he'd been staring at the night before sprang onto the screen. He took out a piece of paper and started scribbling them down. This list he wasn't going to lose hold of.

He gathered up the disks and stuffed them in his bag, then shut the bedroom door behind him. The apartment was empty. "Thanks, Helen!" he shouted, just in case she was around some-where. "One more day and I'll get your old beauty back to you. It runs great. You should enter it in a car show." He waited a second, his hand on the doorknob. When there was no answer, he fished the keys out of his pocket and opened the door into the blaze of Vegas heat.

* * *

"Frankie O'Connor," he muttered. "Where the hell are you?" The list, crumpled on the seat beside him, was stained with coffee now. He'd been driving around in Summerlin, waiting at the gates of the ritzier subdivisions until someone pulled in just ahead of him, then following quickly behind, waving to the half-asleep security guard. He'd found a dusty, rubberbanded roll of twenties under the front seat of the Cadillac, and he'd had to peel off a few at the last place, when the security guard seemed determined to wield some sweating, red-faced authority. The gate had opened quickly enough after that. But that address, like all the others, had yielded nothing except another Hispanic woman who smelled like cleaning supplies. "No es Frankie. No vive aquí," she'd repeated several times and then shut the door firmly. As he walked away, he saw her peering out the window. When he waved, the curtain fell back into place.

He pulled into the parking lot of a 7-Eleven on Sahara, letting the engine idle, to keep the air on, and stared at the giant American flag waving above the car dealership next door. He'd eaten nothing today, unless you counted coffee and a bag of Doritos, and his stomach felt like shit. He leaned his head back against the headrest and watched a woman at the dealership wearing a tight dress and high heels arguing with a greasy-looking, heavyset man, presumably her husband. They were standing near a gleaming black Hummer, the woman gesturing wildly, the man shaking his head. A salesman headed across the parking lot and slapped the husband on the shoulder, holding out a hand to shake, but the woman waved him away and continued yelling at her husband. Huh, thought Brady. That guy ain't getting any tonight.

The cell phone on the seat next to him began vibrating and Brady picked it up. He didn't recognize the number. He pressed the green button and waited. "Mr. Brady?" a female voice said, finally. "It's Ilene."

It was her. It had to be. He recognized her way of speaking, a distinctive tone of half-trepidation, half-flirtatiousness. And besides, he hadn't given his number to anyone else. He paused a second more before responding, then thought, what the hell.

He wasn't having much luck and things couldn't get much worse. "Are you calling from a pay phone?" he said.

"Yes."

"Don't tell me where you are."

"I just wanted to ask you something."

"So spit it out." His stomach was rumbling. "I don't have much time."

"Some people I know are making a lot of money."

He laughed. "In Vegas, really? Okay. So what else is new?"

"Don't laugh! You don't know what I've been — what's going on."

"I'm sorry. Tell me."

"I want to, I just . . . it's so . . ." She was starting to cry. "Do you have a pen?" The connection was breaking up.

He grabbed the crumpled list and a pencil. "Yes."

"9468 High —"

"Ilene? Ilene?" Brady looked at the screen, but it was dark and the phone was silent. "Goddammit," he said, then clutching his gut, jumped out of the car and ran for the door of the 7-Eleven.

* * *

It was 9468 High Sail Court, a huge house in the Lakes. He hoped it was, anyway. Two hours and six addresses later, Brady found himself squinting at the large arched doorway, the perfectly kept lawn that stretched out to the curb, unheard of in Vegas, except in the historic section on Alta Drive and for people who had Mafia-type incomes. No doubt there was a gazebo out back, a pool, a Jacuzzi. The nouveau riche, Brady thought. Right. Even Gatsby had an honorable intention, or a genuine one, at least. In Las Vegas, the greed seemed to feed itself, a monster chomping its mighty jaws on the residents of this hapless, hopeless city, grinding them up and spitting them back out to die in the scorching desert heat. Like Colleen Winters, poor dame. And Lil, he thought, a lump forming in his throat. He glanced up at the sun, starting its slight downward curve toward the west. People weren't meant to live in this part of the world — the only creatures that thrived here were scorpions and lizards, and the black widows that hung from the webs on every shrub in Summerlin. Even the wild burros out in Red Rock Canyon seemed beaten down, heads hanging low, barely energetic enough to scuff a hoof in the red dust.

He swallowed, looking at the house, then closed his eyes and clasped his hands under his chin, praying to the gods of Las Vegas luck. Let Frankie O'Connor open the door.

* * *

It was another maid, though, who came when he rang the bell, a housekeeper, something like that, this one in a short black French maid outfit. Damn, Brady thought. Even the household help is sexy in Vegas.

"Can I help you?" she asked in what sounded like an Eastern European accent. She picked at her cuticle briefly, then glanced at him. "If you're looking for Mr. Nazarian, he isn't home."

Bingo! Brady's palms started to sweat. He stuck his hands in his pockets, trying to look casual. "Actually, I was looking for a friend of mine, Frankie O'Connor. He around?" He grinned. "Nice place you got here. Are you Mrs. Nazarian?"

She smiled, showing a set of small white teeth, a slight gap between the front two. "If you were a friend of Mr. O'Connor's, you would know the answer to that silly question, wouldn't you."

"Frankie's an old friend. Haven't seen him in a while," Brady said, trying not to let his eyes swerve down to her ample cleavage.

"Yah, yah." She pressed a button on the intercom. "Bruno. Come to the main entry, please."

"No, wait," Brady said. He shoved a hand against the door. Behind her he caught a glimpse of another woman walking down the entryway hall, this one in a black lace bra, a thong, and six-inch stripper heels. She looked familiar. Juliet?

"Bruno!" the French maid said again, impatiently this time, pressing the button repeatedly. "You have to have a pass," she said to Brady. "So cut this bullshit. I know what you are here for, but the party doesn't start until eight. Did you send in your picture I.D.?"

Brady pulled out his wallet, thumbing through the myriad cards he had inside. "Okay, okay. Sorry." He was guessing wildly now, trying to figure a new angle. "He told me to say I was a friend, but it's Quinton Samuels who sent me. To talk to Mr. O'Connor." He held up Samuels' card. "He asked me to check on some details for the party tonight."

"Uh huh. Do you have any weapons?" She patted her hands over his chest and belt area, her hands stopping just short of his groin.

"No," he said. Which, for once, was the truth. He'd accidentally left the .32 in the glove box of Helen's Caddy.

She pressed a manicured fingernail against his chest. "I don't believe a word you are saying, but you look kind of —" She leaned toward him. "Hungry. So why don't you come in."

He felt his breath go out all at once. "Thank you," he said, beads of sweat popping out on his forehead. He knew he sounded overly grateful, as if she'd just offered him a blow job. "Awfully hot out today," he said, to redeem himself.

She rolled her eyes. "He's down the hall," she said, then led the way in.

* * *

The house was probably eight thousand square feet, he estimated, the floors slick marble tile, and Persian rugs a lot bigger than Helen's. He rubbed his cheek, wondering if it still looked like he'd slept on the floor all night. They glided down the long hall for what seemed like forever, the French maid's heels clicking. A tiny white dog scampered out of an adjoining hallway and the woman bent over to pick it up. She was wearing a frilly petticoat underneath her dress and not much else.

"What's your name?" Brady said.

"Anya," she said.

"Oh yeah? Like Tanya? Without the T?" He laughed, trying to peer into the rooms on each side of the hall as they passed. A bathroom with a shiny whirlpool tub and thick towels, a room that looked like a sports bar, complete with a stripper pole and neon Budweiser signs, and beyond that, a black and red dungeon. A dungeon? He glanced in, trying to gather as many details as he could. Yes, metal restraints on the far wall, handcuffs dangling, a black padded table, a glass cabinet filled with cattails and flogs. A swing. Not exactly your ordinary Vegas mansion. He glanced up at the ceiling of the long hall. A video camera, its black eye pointed directly at him.

"Coming?" Anya said. She gestured into another room with mirrored walls and a fake fireplace, and Frankie O'Connor, in all his slim elegance, stood up from the couch to greet him.

* * *

Brady pushed his foot around in the thick white carpet. "This must be hard to keep clean," he said. "Red wine or blood? Dang.

You'd have to replace the whole thing."

O'Connor smiled, thin skin stretched over his still-firm jaw-line, and gestured at a chair. "Have a seat. Luckily we employ a good cleaning service." He winked at Anya.

She smiled and ducked out of the room, then poked her head back in. "Let me know if you need anything," she said, raising her eyebrows for a moment under her thick blond bangs.

"Oh, we will," O'Connor said, sitting back down, then turned to Brady. "Like the furniture? It's from the old Stardust."

Brady glanced at the couch. The upholstery looked like it had been cleaned about ten thousand times. There were elbow prints on the armrests of the leather chairs. "It's great. Really something."

O'Connor nodded. "This house is a marvel. The old and the new, all spun together. Past and the present. The poor and the rich."

"Who's poor?" Brady asked. "Looks like you've got everything here." He glanced at the wet bar by the fireplace. "Women, cameras. A great view." He gestured at the window. Outside, a truck had just pulled up and a group of Hispanic men jumped out and stood talking and gesturing at a fat palm tree growing near the side gate.

"So Samuels sent you over, eh?" O'Connor picked up a tumbler of clear liquid. "Grey Goose. Want some?"

"No thanks, stomach's acting up," Brady said. He tried to

smile. Something about O'Connor's cool, dry, paper-thin skin gave him the creeps. "Yeah, he —" Brady paused, then pulled a lie out of his ass. "He wants a special room. For tonight. He said some of the members of the School Board are coming, as his guests, and they don't want any cameras. Nazarian would agree, wouldn't he? It's all about the money, right? And these guys can pay."

For a millisecond O'Connor's eyes went blank, and Brady knew he had him. Inside, he crowed. He had guessed right. "So how much is this place making these days? Couple million a month?"

O'Connor had regained his composure, began talking as though Brady were in on the whole thing. "Hell of a lot more than that. Seven and a half million. We pay the girls ten thousand each — per month — and the rest is just upkeep on the house. We have three hundred thousand members now. Technology these days. It's a wonder."

Brady nodded, and O'Connor leaned forward, swirling his vodka around in his glass. "People love this stuff. This room is the only one in the house that's not camera'd up. Members can log on to the site, watch five gorgeous girls doing it all day long, and all night. In the shower. In bed. During playtime." He laughed. "Throw a dildo into a group of five porn stars and everybody has fun. Vegas Voyeur Club. What a great idea. Any dope with a computer can have his own personal peep show.

And the parties. Come watch your favorite porn star doing a photo shoot! Nazarian is a genius. And it's not even illegal." He smiled his frigid smile.

"Shit," said Brady. "Can I come? To the party, I mean?"

"Tonight is Nazarian's night. Naked Jake is bringing his sex toys. And Carl Pistel's coming. He's going to do some of the photography himself. For Nazarian, of course. He wants his own personal video, two Asian chicks getting tied up and spanked." He laughed drily. "It's the midnight special. Two for the price of one."

"So what about the room? Should I tell Samuels it's a go?"

"You've got the money?"

Brady cleared his throat, wondering who else was in on this scheme, or had been. Creamer? Fat Andy Sachman? Joseph Don Walker? Samuels, obviously, even though it had been just a hunch. This was way more than fake bills or fixed decks at a poker table. This was real money. Real, fat-ass stacks of bills, piling up like dirty dishes. "Definitely. It's in the trunk, outside. I'll go get it."

O'Connor stood up. "I'll go with you," he said, smoothly. He set his vodka on the mantel and patted Brady on the shoulder. "We'll walk through the gallery." He padded across the room and opened a door on the other side. "Take a look, why don't you. No charge."

Brady peered inside. A row of portraits lined the wall of

another high-ceilinged room. The lovely Anya. Juliet. Huh. That was no surprise. A bunch of other women he didn't recognize. He scanned the pictures as they walked to the far end of the room. And Ilene. *Ilene.* In the two-by-three portrait, the slender woman was propped on her elbows on a fur rug, high-heeled feet crossed up over her naked ass, light red hair piled on top of her head, a few sexy strands dangling down. His eyes went back to her tits and ass. Jesus. Who would have thought she had all that going on under her faded jeans and T-shirt? Her almond-shaped eyes smiled suggestively at him.

Colleen Winters' beautiful granddaughter. What had Colleen done, ratted on her own grandchild? Threatened her? Begged her not to do it anymore? Something had happened, and now Colleen was dead.

Guilt. It was always guilt. No wonder Ilene was looking so frail these days.

Chapter Seven

By Vu Tran

They entered a long, narrow hallway. O'Connor gestured toward the green door at the far end. "This way to the front. A shortcut." He patted Brady on the shoulder again, as if he were consoling him about something, and made his way leisurely down the hallway.

Brady followed a few steps behind, his eyes drawn again to the walls, lined now with oil paintings in gold gilt frames. Nazarian apparently was a fan of nineteenth century Orientalism . . . a naked boy standing entwined in a giant snake . . . a naked slave-girl for sale at the market, gorgeous and prodded by prospective buyers . . . naked, porcelain-skinned women lounging in smoky harems, bathed by black servants. Back in college

— his one year at UNLV — Brady had seen shit like this in an art history class. Shit like this you tend to remember, even if the class bored you to tears. Now they lent this place a whiff of elegance. Sordid elegance anyway. Brady knew full well that no matter the place, the century, or the art, at the end of the day tits were tits and ass was ass. We only see what we're looking for, and we always look for what we desire.

O'Connor walked in silence. Brady considered the lie he'd have to offer him once they reached his car. He could have simply forgotten the money. Or perhaps he'd grabbed the wrong suitcase. A swift punch in the throat was a good option too.

The green door opened into a dimly lighted library. What books did people here read? Were these books even real? O'Connor continued his patient stroll, saying nothing. When they passed the coffee table, Brady swiped the tiny glass ashtray and slipped it into his pocket. They reached another door that opened into what appeared to be a game room. A pool table. A card table. A table stacked with an assortment of expensive-looking cameras. He could only imagine the pictures they'd taken.

Then, in the middle of the room, O'Connor stopped. He stood facing a gigantic French window that framed the back grounds of the mansion and a swimming pool glittering in the late-afternoon sun. The front driveway was nowhere in sight.

"Are you good at what you do?" O'Connor asked without turning around. His voice had lost its casual lilt. He seemed an altogether different man now — his thinness no longer frail or papery, but rather an accentuation of his great height. He was nearly a foot taller than Brady, and standing in the window's cascading sunlight, his long shadow loomed across the room.

"Come again?" Brady said, palming the ashtray in his pocket. He realized there were two doors here: the one they had just walked through, still gaping open, and another he nearly missed that stood flush with the crimson wall, painted the exact same color.

"You're the private detective, are you not?"

"Were you expecting one?"

O'Connor finally turned to him with an amused frown, like one he'd give a mischievous child. "Come now — we both know you're not here to carry out some silly transaction for Samuels. He would never send anyone but that Asian lawyer of his. And you, sir, are neither Asian nor a lawyer. Besides, as soon as you walked into my parlor, I could smell the curiosity on you. A drunk baby could have sniffed you out. Tell me, how long have you been doing this sort of work?"

"Are you trying to hurt my feelings, Mr. O'Connor?"

"I don't give a damn about your feelings. It just fascinates me when people think they can outsmart people they're unequipped to outsmart." O'Connor reached for the phone on the desk beside him. "Hello, Thomas," he said into the receiver. "Is he in a good mood? Good. Tell him that Samuels' detective has gotten lost here."

Tommy. Why was Brady not surprised that he'd be seeing Tommy again? What role would *Thomas* be playing this time? Brady had barely exchanged four words with the son of a bitch, but the guy had become a figurehead now for everyone he'd met so far in this ridiculous game. Everyone had their role, didn't they? It struck Brady that even he had been playing a role, though he was damned if he knew what it was. At this point, were it still in his possession, he would have gladly given up the fourteen thousand dollars Samuels paid him to know.

He said to O'Connor, who had taken off his jacket and draped it carefully over a chair: "Before your guys come and escort me to the desert, just answer me one question. Why did Nazarian have Colleen Winters killed? What — did she take her grand-daughter away from him? Does Nazarian enjoy young flesh so much that he'd have a sixty-seven-year-old woman killed to keep her quiet, to keep her from protecting her own grandchild?"

O'Connor chuckled. "That's three or four questions there, Mr. Detective. And they're all, unfortunately, the wrong ones."

"And how about Samuels? Does he know about what happened? Or does Nazarian distract him with enough jailbait to keep him away from the truth? Was Ilene that jailbait?"

O'Connor looked at Brady sharply now and his voice became hard: "You know, you and Samuels might do very different things for a living, but you both have one thing in common

— you're terribly sentimental. You cry for the poor old woman and the innocent young girl, and you think only the old rich men are evil and have people killed on a whim. You think men like me and Mr. Nazarian have no heart, no morals whatsoever. Do you think just because we're in the business of being rich that we don't care if people live or die?"

"I've heard of the things Nazarian is capable of."

"He is a *good* man," O'Connor said loudly. "He just happens to have a lot of money, and people can't handle that much wealth on a person without assigning him a few ills. It makes hating and envying him easier. But Mr. Nazarian is eighty-nine years old. He has no family to speak of, all the money in the world, and at most four or five years left on Earth to enjoy it. Trust me, he's not going to spend those years creating problems for himself. Yes, he has his odd habits — his predilections, if you will. But Mr. Nazarian is not a bad man."

Brady wanted to laugh at him, to ask him how much money he'd made off the Ancient Billionaire Mariner — how much money it took to help him drink his own Kool-Aid.

But O'Connor suddenly took off his shoes, then his socks, which he neatly stuffed into the shoes. Then, with all the casualness in the world, he unbuckled his belt, unzipped his pants, and let them fall to the floor. He glanced at Brady. "You might want to take off your clothes, Mr. Detective."

"What? What the hell for?"

"You obviously have many questions. Do you want the answers?"

"What the fuck are you gonna make me do to get them?"

O'Connor sighed impatiently. He nodded at the crimson door. "Behind this closed door is Mr. Nazarian. Through that open door is your freedom. Right now, you have two choices. You can leave and make your way safely off these premises. I will not stop you. My men will not so much as look at you as you drive away, never to return again, all your burning questions still unanswered. Or you can stay and ask Mr. Nazarian anything you want, all the questions which — quite frankly — you've been so very bad at answering yourself. But if you do stay, you will do exactly as I tell you."

O'Connor stood there in his blue boxers, waiting patiently for a response. His legs looked like white stilts.

Brady glanced at the open door, then suddenly thought of Lil. He remembered the first time they met decades ago at headquarters and she had held the door open for him and then slapped him playfully on the ass as he passed by, her eyes as wide as her lipstick grin. Brady gave O'Connor a long look. "So what — *all* my clothes?"

"Even your watch. Mr. Nazarian requires it."

They both proceeded to undress, O'Connor neatly folding every article of clothing and placing it on the desk, Brady simply sloughing off everything onto the floor.

O'Connor walked to the crimson door and knocked on it once. It crept open, and standing there, utterly naked with his prick dangling out of a red pubic forest, was Tommy. He glanced at Brady without emotion or recognition, then nodded at O'Connor before opening the door wider and standing aside.

Inside the windowless room, amid the sounds of Hank Williams singing "Hey Good Lookin'," a poker game was in progress. Four young women and four older men — including the Ancient Mariner himself — were playing, and there was not a stitch of clothing in sight. The women were quite attractive, and the men were thankfully sitting down. It was apparently a serious poker game, with chip stacks and bricks of cash in front of every player, many of whom were expertly shuffling their chips and following the hand in play with sober interest. No one looked up when O'Connor and Brady walked in.

Nick Nazarian sat facing the door, hunched over and contemplating his hand, his hoary chest baring two pale, sagging breasts as dejected-looking as his expression. After a long moment, his bony fingers grabbed a stack of chips and pushed them into the pot. "I call," he announced to the fat man across the table, whose ass Brady could see spilling over the edges of his leather chair.

"You win, sir," the fat man grumbled and flung his cards into the muck.

Nazarian's face burst into a gleeful smile, and he finally looked up at Brady. "Skinny here always thinks he can bluff me!" He spoke with a loud, measured drawl. Gathering his big pot, he went on, "So you're Samuels' *private dick*, huh?" He grinned knowingly at the amply breasted blonde to his right, who took a moment to understand the joke and then giggled into her cards. Nazarian turned to O'Connor, who stood mute by the wall, holding his privates in one hand. "Frankie, meet Samuels' dick!" He snickered loudly, and while the men at the table seemed impatient for the game to continue, the women began laughing.

Brady did not return their humor. He couldn't tell if this "game" was a way for the old man to get off or simply the casual reality of things around here. In any case, the outlandishness of everything was only making him more impatient. He said, "I was told you would explain some things for me, Mr. Nazarian."

"Why sure. Mr. *Brady*, right? I suppose someone owes you an explanation at this point, Mr. Brady. Might as well be me."

Brady hardly knew where to start. After everything that had happened to him over the past few days, this all seemed too easy now. The poker game had stopped, and everyone was looking at him, a couple of the women eyeing him up and down with a smile. Finally, he said, "What happened to Colleen Winters?"

"The inevitable happened to her, that's what. But I know what you're thinking. And no, I didn't do nothing to her. And Samuels didn't either. He loved her too much. I'm as old as a goddamn tortoise, and half the time I can't even find my own prick. But I still know people. And Quinton Samuels — idiot friend of mine that he is — never stopped loving that woman. Sometimes loved her more than his own good sense. Yeah, you play poker with a person for forty years, and you tend to know when their good sense leaves them."

Nazarian was eyeing a poker chip that he was cascading down the knuckles of his hand. He looked his age but still had the agile hands of a magician. And it was clear he loved to talk, that his mind had not lost any of its clarity or vitality.

"So who killed her?" Brady asked him.

Nazarian looked at him for a moment, then made a gesture at his fellow poker players. They immediately stood and began making their way out of the room, the three middle-aged men whispering playfully to the women as they all filed past Brady. Only O'Connor — and the young blonde next to Nazarian — remained. She was playing with her poker chips, and still intermittently staring at Brady's cock.

After the door closed behind Tommy, Nazarian continued in his patient drawl: "You see, Mr. Brady, Colleen Winters spent most of her life feeding off sugar daddies like Samuels. And when the well ran dry, she began stealing from people like me. I caught her three years ago scamming jackpots at one of my smaller casinos. I would've punished her good if Samuels hadn't stepped in to save her, as I figured he would. So, for his sake, I allowed her to be in debt to me. And unfortunately her only method of payment was her beautiful granddaughter. Now, mind you, I never did nothing to that girl but treat her as a favorite. She was my most popular girl here, after all. But after a year or two she apparently didn't like the work no more. And I guess I can't blame her. Fucking in front of old horny men can get a little degrading, I suppose. But a debt's a debt, right? Her grandma insisted the girl stay, so the girl decided to leave town. And that's when Colleen, as always, got desperate. She threatened to kill the girl if she didn't come back. Love among family can sometimes turn ugly, no? I'm kinda glad I never *had* a family. Anyway, the girl's boyfriend — Axel, is it? Your biker friend? — he jumped in to protect his girl. And like any good born-again Christian would, he went alone to her grandmother's house to show her the error of her ways. He shoved her underwear down her throat and then beat the old woman with a closed fist. Just to scare her, he thought, to keep her away from his girl. Only the boy didn't think she would die from the beating. A stupid boy. Well, anyway, the girl found out about what he did for her, and that's when she cut herself. Out of guilt for her part, I suppose. I found out all about it because the girl decided to do herself in right here, under my roof. A pity — such beautiful wrists."

The old man gestured at O'Connor to get him a glass of water. He was staring at the empty poker table and looked tired. Or maybe he was suddenly sad.

Brady didn't know what to say. He remembered Axel a few days ago and realized how much of an acting job it was, though the boy's fear was apparently very real. What must he have thought when Brady called him up for information about the very thing he was trying so desperately to hide?

Nazarian could see Brady's confusion. "It's a shame, isn't it?" the old man said, after drinking his water. "That the people you love end up doing the worst things to you? Maybe that's why I never tried to love anything or anyone. Shouldn't make me a monster, should it? Especially if people who *do* love others end up screwing them over anyway?"

"I don't understand," Brady began, but then held his breath. Nazarian's last few words made him human all of a sudden, despite what he was admitting about himself. Why not just trust the old man at this point? What did Brady have to lose that he was not already risking by simply being here? He said, "If Samuels didn't do anything to Colleen Winters and genuinely hired me to get information about it, why set me up? Why follow me, and have me taped, and fuck with my head? That stuff in Laughlin. My friend in the trunk . . . my friend who . . . And all those videos in those apartments, Mr. Nazarian. Of the funeral. Of Andy Sachman getting shot. Of Mr. O'Connor here. What does any of this have to do with me?"

The old man held up his hand, shaking his head with disappointment. "I don't know about all that. Samuels goes overboard. Doesn't trust nobody, least of all your type, Mr. Brady. He came to me about Colleen, and I told him about the granddaughter and her boyfriend, 'cause that's all I knew. He wanted their heads on a platter, but they had both disappeared, and I didn't know where to. Eh, I'm too old for this kinda stuff. Maybe I shouldn't have told him anything. Thing is, Colleen was involved with some very bad folks. If her granddaughter's boyfriend hadn't killed her first, those folks would've did it eventually. And you see, she was helping them steal from Samuels. Problem was, he didn't want to think his dear Colleen would do that to him."

"I told you he was sentimental," O'Connor suddenly said from his spot by the wall. He'd been listening with interest, though Brady couldn't tell what was new or old information to him. The blonde, however, seemed completely oblivious to the conversation. She was continuously shuffling the deck of cards, staring off into space.

"So what you're saying," Brady said to Nazarian, "is that Samuels hired me after he already knew exactly what had happened? That Axel had killed Colleen? That Colleen was in on all the scams against him?"

The old man nodded. "He hired you to find out more about the people stealing from him. But he also wanted you to find Axel for him. And you did."

"Mr. Nazarian, why are you telling me all this?"

"Because you're an honest man, Mr. Brady. Kinda stupid, but honest nevertheless. You wouldn't have risked coming here, to the house of a man like me, if you weren't anything but honest. I've lived a long life, a good part of it lying to people, and what I've learned is that we wear all kinds of disguises, every single second of the day. Even when we're alone. And we'll only be truly honest to each other, and to ourselves, when we're forced to. That's why I have my poker game the way I do."

He reached over and cupped one of the blonde's breasts. She seemed to barely notice him touching her. "It's nice to have this around, of course. But really, when you're buck naked, you have nothing to hide behind. Sure, you can still bluff with your eyes and your words, but at least in this room, things are a bit more . . . *pure*. Haven't you been thinking and acting differently these last ten minutes, Mr. Brady, standing there completely naked before me?"

He drank again from his glass of water, which O'Connor promptly refilled.

"But the thing is, you've put me in the goddamnedest position. Now you know too much. Can't say I've done anything wrong here, but the cops you'll go to may not agree. I got a few of them under my belt, but unfortunately not all of them. If anything, it'd be bad publicity. And that puts me in a bind. The goddamnedest position really. I should do something bad to you, Mr. Brady. But the truth is, I feel a little guilty for my part in this whole thing — what with Colleen getting killed and the girl trying to off herself. And I did provide Samuels with all the tools to play around with you. He needed my expertise. I am, after all, a creator of fantasy." He made a sweeping gesture at everything around him, his mischievous grin returning. "So, to relieve my guilt, I'm gonna make you a deal." He looked down at the cash in front of him and grabbed four bricks. He nudged them across the poker table toward Brady. "Here's two hundred grand. Take it, go home, keep your mouth shut. Forget any of this happened. You let me handle Samuels."

Brady looked at the four bricks of cash, each as thick as a Bible. This all seemed unreal, a cruel trick perhaps. He glanced at Nazarian, and then at O'Connor, who was staring at the cash with something like mourning.

"There's still a lot I don't understand here, sir."

"Enough questions, Mr. Brady. I'm old and tired and you've interrupted my poker game for long enough. Take the money, and take my advice: Forget this all happened."

Brady took a step toward the table. It occurred to him that he could retire with this money and never have to deal with these kinds of people ever again. But then could he really ever forget them?

Suddenly, the blonde awoke from her stupor and turned to him, and with a wry smile, she said, "Take the money, sailor. It's not about honesty or integrity. It's about necessity."

She glanced down at her left breast, the one Nazarian had cupped, and wiped at it a couple of times with her fingers, as though she were wiping away a stain.

* * *

As he drove away from the mansion, Brady could not yet breathe a sigh of relief. He asked himself whether men like Nazarian and Samuels — and even O'Connor for that matter — had so much money and, more importantly, so much intelligence that they couldn't end up justifying anything to themselves — and to others.

He still didn't know what to make of the old man's story, but it was convoluted enough to be believable. Samuels found out somehow that Brady was friends with Axel and would go to him for information. He had Brady followed from the very beginning and must have nabbed Axel right after Brady met with him west of town. He probably grabbed Ilene soon after that. God knows what he was planning to do to them if Brady hadn't found them at the apartment. Samuels' story about Colleen in his suite was both genuine and a ruse. He was confessing his history with the old woman, his feelings for her, but was also building an elaborate scenario to distract Brady. In case Axel's body was ever dug up in the desert, Brady would suspect Samuels' enemies, not Samuels himself. Putting Brady on the trail of guys like Andy Sachman, and then killing them, was a way of framing them for the murders of Colleen and, preemptively, of Axel himself. Everything had been a way to distract, to confuse. Creamer the lawyer had been telling the truth about the set-up. Laughlin was a wild goose chase. Juliet was no more Ilene's sister than Brady was. And Tommy was probably the one making all those mysterious phone calls, leading Brady astray, etc, etc. . . . And all of this because Samuels wanted to avenge the death of a lover who had, in fact, betrayed him. Was that foolish as hell, or the most romantic thing in the world?

As he hopped onto I-15, Brady kept his hand on the duffel bag in the passenger seat, fondling the shape of the cash bricks inside. There were two more things he needed to do before he could forget this all happened.

* * *

When he knocked on the door of Samuels' suite, creepy Kevin greeted him with genuine surprise in his eyes.

"Let me see Samuels," Brady said. "I have a delivery for him."

Kevin glanced at the duffel bag. Brady handed it to him and then put his hands on the wall to wait for the pat-down.

Samuels was reading a book on the couch. He looked, as always, like he'd just come from the tennis courts. When Brady appeared at the edge of the living room, he looked up from his book and appeared to ponder the universe. He slowly took off his glasses. "Where have you been, Mr. Brady? I've been worried."

"I'm okay now. Thank you for your concern. I apologize, but I had to lose you first before I could find you."

Samuels smiled at Kevin, as though Kevin might be in on the joke. He turned back to Brady. "I don't think I understand."

Kevin brought over the duffel bag, which Samuels unzipped. He looked inside, and for the first time probably in a very long time, he could not hide his confusion.

Brady said, "I went to see your friend, Mr. Nazarian. He explained a few things. And he offered me this money to keep quiet. If you don't believe me, then you can call O'Connor yourself. He said you were a sentimental and untrusting man."

Samuels could only sit there. His silence confirmed everything.

"That's two hundred grand there. I took fourteen of it, what you had originally paid me and then taken from me. I'll put it towards a new car, since mine has probably been gutted back in Laughlin. Maybe I can also buy a new poker table and take up the game with some old friends. You'd appreciate that, right? In any case, the rest of that money is yours as a payment."

"A payment for what, Mr. Brady?"

"For Axel's life. He didn't mean to kill Colleen. He was just looking out for his girl. Isn't that the same thing you've been doing for the past forty years?"

Samuels grinned, almost sadly. He seemed to appreciate the

analogy. He took out a brick of cash and peered at it tiredly as if it was some unwanted thing that he suddenly had found in his possession again. He let it fall from his hand back into the duffel bag.

"That might not be a terrible amount of money to a man like you," Brady continued, "but I'm sure you know how much it is to a man like me. I promise you I won't say anything more about any of this. My payment to you should give you some faith in that promise."

Samuels gazed at him for a long, cold moment. Then he zipped up the duffel bag and embraced it in his lap. "Okay then, Mr. Brady. Kevin will show you out."

"One last thing. I want to know where she is."

"Where *who* is?"

"You know who I'm talking about."

Samuels looked genuinely confused for a second, but then recognition dawned on his face. He took the napkin from the coffee table and wrote something down on it. He handed it to Kevin, who delivered it to Brady.

"You are an honest man, Mr. Brady," Samuels said, shaking his head with a smile.

"That's what people tell me anyway."

* * *

The napkin read: *Binion's Horseshoe Casino, Room 225.*

How appropriate, Brady thought. And utterly predictable.

When he knocked on the room, no one answered. He knocked a few more times and waited. Nothing. He decided to try the bar.

He was not surprised to see her sitting by herself, martini in hand and plopping Tomolives into her mouth, her bright red nails flashing in the floodlights. She seemed utterly unconcerned that she was sitting in the middle of a popular casino where anyone could see her. But Lil had never been an inconspicuous person.

Brady thought it would be easy. But then he walked up to her and she turned and saw him and looked at him like he had shot her and in her cigarette-raspy drawl said, "Daniel?" Only then did he feel it like a punch in the chest. She raised her hand to her face when she said his name, as though she were hiding her face, or shading herself from a blinding light, or simply afraid that Brady might touch her. She wore tight jeans and a flowery pink blouse, her make-up and hair and nails all perfectly done as always — not a single scratch on her. If Brady had seen just a bandage on her head or something, he could have felt at least a moment of relief. Instead, he only felt heartbroken.

He sat down beside her. "You were in on all this?" he asked her quietly.

Lil could only stare at the scratched surface of the bar. She downed her martini in a single gulp and then looked squarely at him. "Not at the beginning, Daniel. I promise you. That bartender — Tommy? At the bar here that night? He accosted me in the parking garage after you left and brought me over to Samuels' suite. *Forced* me to go. That Asian lawyer was there too. They knew everything about me. Everything. Samuels said if I didn't help him, he'd ruin me. You know I did some shady stuff in the past, Daniel. You knew what was hanging over my head. And I had debts too. Bad debts."

"We all have our debts, Lil."

"But I was in more shit than you can imagine."

"Trust me, I can imagine anything now. Did he threaten to kill you?"

"Well, no. But he was going to ruin me."

"So — how much did he offer you?"

"Daniel!"

"How much, Lil?"

She was silent for a moment, then gestured at the bartender for another drink. "Fifty thousand." She looked at him. "That would have paid off all my debts. I would have had a little left over to rent a place in Northern Cali somewhere, away from this town and all my ex-husbands and all those stupid memories. *Finally* — after a lifetime here. I could live by the forest and the ocean. Breathe clean air and, for once, be debt-free. That's the only thing I've ever wanted. Can't you understand for me, Daniel?"

Brady shook his head slowly. He called the bartender over
and asked for a shot of whiskey. "You know, I mourned you.
And I thought it was all my fault. For days, all I could think
about was seeing the back of your head and your hair all messy
as you lay there in the trunk of my car. You remember what
you said to me when we put the cuffs on that gang twenty years
ago? You said, 'We're the good guys and they're the bad guys,
and the bad guys always lose.' "

The bartender poured the whiskey, and Brady picked up the
shot glass with a mix of nostalgia and acceptance. "Last time I
had a sip of alcohol, Reagan was president and I still believed
in the future." He downed the shot. Then he said to the bartender, "The lady will take care of it." He stood from the bar
and patted Lil on the hand. "Have a good rest of your life in
California, Miss Lilian."

She grabbed his hand and said, "So you forgive me, right?
Please say you forgive me."

"I guess I have to. What's there left to do at this point?" He
pulled his hand out of hers. "But for the rest of my life, I never
want to see you again."

He walked away from the bar and made his way toward the
exit. Outside on Fremont Street, the massive mesh ceiling was
trembling. Any minute now the light show would begin and
flood Fremont with vertiginous computer images and deafening
music. He was walking fast now. He didn't want to get caught

in the crowds of awestruck tourists. They were there for a show.
He felt sorry for them.

THE END

H. LEE BARNES

A Vietnam veteran, former casino dealer, and law enforcement officer, H. Lee Barnes has taught at the College of Southern Nevada since 1997. He has published more than thirty short stories and is author of the collections *Gunning for Ho* (2000), *Talk to Me, James Dean* (2004), and *Minimal Damage* (2007), as well as the novel *The Lucky* (2003) and a work of nonfiction, *Dummy up and Deal* (2005). He was inducted into the Nevada Writers Hall of Fame in November 2009.

JOHN H. IRSFELD

Raised and educated in Texas, John Irsfeld is a longtime UNLV English professor and member of the Nevada Writers Hall of Fame. He is the author of several novels and story collections, including *Night Moves* (2007), *Radio Elvis and Other Stories* (2002), *Rats Alley* (1987) *Little Kingdoms* (1976) and *Coming Through* (1975).

BRIAN ROUFF

Brian Rouff was born in Detroit, raised in Southern California, and has lived in Las Vegas since 1981, which makes him a longtimer by local standards. When he's not writing articles, screenplays and Las Vegas-based novels such as *Dice Angel* (2002) and *Money Shot* (2004), he runs Imagine Marketing, an advertising and public relations firm in Henderson.

LEAH BAILLY

A playwright, fiction writer and journalist, Canadian Leah
Bailly has just returned from several years abroad, including
extensive sojourns in Africa and India. Her work has appeared
in publications such as *Prism*, *subTerrain*, *Room*, *Forget* and
Parlour Magazine, and her nonfiction was recently nominated
for an Alberta Literary Award for travel writing. Her play titled
Some Reckless Abandon (based on early travels to Latin America)
was performed on a seven-city tour across the United States and
Canada. Leah is pursuing an MFA in fiction at UNLV, where
she is deputy editor of the literary journal *Witness*. In 2010, she
will begin a four-month writing project with Journalists for
Human Rights in Sierra Leone.

JOHN L. SMITH

A fourth-generation Nevadan, John L. Smith is an award-winning columnist for the *Las Vegas Review-Journal* and the author of eleven nonfiction books, including *Running Scared: The Life and Treacherous Times of Las Vegas Casino King Steve Wynn*, *No Limit: The Rise and Fall of Bob Stupak and Las Vegas' Stratosphere Tower*, and *Of Rats and Men: Oscar Goodman's Life from Mob Mouthpiece to Mayor of Las Vegas*. His latest book is *Amelia's Long Journey*, a collection of his newspaper columns about his daughter's battle with cancer.

CONSTANCE FORD

Constance Ford is the original Schaeffer Fellow at UNLV, where she earned her Ph.D. in English. Previously, she earned an MA in fiction from Hollins University, and in 2001 received the Melanie Hook Rice Award. Ford's short stories have been published in several literary magazines. Her story "Little Bird" was a finalist for the 2005 Nelson Algren Award. She is a full-time instructor at the College of Southern Nevada, and is putting the finishing touches on her debut novel, for which she was awarded the Nevada Arts Council Artist Fellowship Award in 2009.

VU TRAN

Vu Tran was born in Saigon, Vietnam, and raised in Oklahoma. His stories have appeared in *The Best American Mystery Stories 2009*, *The O. Henry Prize Stories 2007*, *The Southern Review*, *Glimmer Train*, *Fence*, and other publications. He is a graduate of the Iowa Writers' Workshop and was a Schaeffer Fellow in Fiction at UNLV, where he currently teaches literature and creative writing. Tran received a 2009 Whiting Writers' Award, a prestigious annual honor recognizing ten young writers for their extraordinary talent and promise. His first novel, *This or Any Desert*, is forthcoming from WW. Norton & Company.

GEOFF SCHUMACHER, EDITOR

Geoff Schumacher is an author, columnist, book editor and newspaper executive. He was a reporter, editorial writer, and city editor for the *Las Vegas Sun* for ten years and editor of *Las Vegas CityLife* for three years. He founded and edited the *Las Vegas Mercury*. Today he is the director of community publications for Stephens Media and writes a weekly column for the *Las Vegas Review-Journal*. He is the editor of CityLife Books, an imprint of Stephens Press. Schumacher has authored two works of history: *Howard Hughes: Power, Paranoia & Palace Intrigue* (2008) and *Sun, Sin & Suburbia: An Essential History of Modern Las Vegas* (2004).